Dylan. A

EASTER Island

DYLAN A.

ISBN 978-1-387-08895-9

CHAPTER 1

March 17th 2018

10:00 AM

"Officer Browden, have you done your sweep through section 6B yet?" Another officer spoke into the receiver. "Officer Browden?" She called again.

"Tyreese isn't here." A young, tall man in a blue police uniform said as he made his way to the coffee table. He tipped the pot, and poured a small stream of dark liquid into a Styrofoam cup. It steamed from the surface. The strong smell from the coffee beans filled the room as sunlight filtered inside through the caged windows. The grey, brick walls were dull and cool. The dark cement floor added to the dimness of the atmosphere.

"What do you mean he isn't here?" The female officer questioned.

"I haven't seen him today. I don't think he came in for work." The man held the cup to his mouth with one hand while the other hand rested on the edge of the table.

"Well, wouldn't he have called in sick or something?"

"Haha, since when does Tyreese Browden ever follow the rules?" The officer laughed.

"Yeah, right. Well…mind going up to do his sweep for me then?"

"No problem." The officer gulped down the last of the coffee then tossed the cup lightly into the nearest trash can.

He came to the elevator and swiped his card through the metal track on the scanner. The small, red light jumped to green as the elevator doors unlocked. They slid open in a slow, mechanical type way. Officer Philips entered and pressed the button for the 6th floor.

The female officer, Officer Braidy, made her way into the lounge. She had short cut dirty blonde hair—almost brown. A round, black birthmark sat on the edge of her chin. She didn't wear any face makeup, but her nails were painted black. Three other cops sat in chairs with newspapers and coffee cups in their hands. Braidy walked in and shut the door softly behind her with one hand.

"Have any of you guys seen Browden today?" She asked.

"No ma'am. Haven't seen him. Did you need me to do his sweep?" A broad shouldered officer with a raspy voice answered back.

"I've got Philips on it. But thanks for offering." She had her hand on the door handle, about to leave, when a static sound came through the speaker on her walkie-talkie.

"…Officer Braidy, we have a problem." Officer Philips' voice spoke through the speaker.

The three officers closed their newspapers and sat up in their chairs.

"…What is it? Are you okay?" Braidy spoke back.

"I'm fine. But, Zando…he's gone. He isn't in his cell!"

"Stay right there, we're coming up!"

12:00 PM

The entrance hall was large. The front and side walls were made entirely of mosaic glass. Each square panel was detailed with engraved, glossy patterns that shimmered in the sunlight. The walls stood twelve feet high—twelve foot ceilings. A large, round FBI logo, extremely detailed with white stars and bold letters, covered a portion of the white marble floor. A long, black wooden desk sat at the head of the room with a few receptionists standing behind it. Silver brass elevator doors sat to the right of the desk, while a set of escalator stairs stood to the left. Large, artificial palm trees were placed in each corner of the room while a giant rectangular water fountain covered a part of the floor unoccupied by the FBI logo.

Two people walked through the heavily secured front doors. Two uniformed guards stepped aside, allowing the two people to pass through. They walked simultaneously, moving their legs and arms in the same motions. The man was dressed in a black wool pea coat with matching slacks and shoes. He had dark brown hair, medium length, and a shortly cut beard. A large, golden shield badge was clipped to the folded collar of his coat. The name on the badge read *Lieutenant Fischer*. The woman walking next to him wore a longer black coat that stopped just above her knees, with tall high heeled boots on her feet. She had a smaller badge clipped to her own coat that read *Forensics Agent Berns*. Her light blonde hair glistened in the spring-time sunlight; it hung past her shoulders and down past the back of her neck. It was neatly straightened.

Their shoes clicked on the white tiled surface until it changed to the soft rubber of the ascending escalator. It lifted them up to the second floor—more white tiled floor. The hallway was wide, with another set of escalator stairs and several blurred glass doors. They made their way to the first door, just to the left of the next escalator. Dennis pushed it open with his right hand and held it in place for Amber to walk inside first. The door swung closed as Dennis and Amber took their seats at a long hardwood conference table. Several other men and women dressed in suits occupied the remainder of the seats.

Commander Layton stood at the head of the table with a large presentation screen behind him. He was dressed a lot more casually than the agents; he wore a white button down shirt with the sleeves rolled up and the neck unbuttoned. Rather than black slacks, he wore dark blue jeans with a white leather belt. His head was shaved smooth and shiny. An expensive looking silver watch decorated his left wrist.

"Okay, welcome everybody. As we all know, it has been exactly 8 months since Lieutenant Fischer and Agent Berns returned from Bermuda. We have our court hearing in a few days and this can either make or break us. We're not sure how the public is going to feel about our story…I'm not even sure how I feel about. So, we could bend the truth a little bit to make it sound more "realistic", or we could just tell everything as is. Any suggestions?" The Commander spoke.

"Well…while I was there, I documented everything." Dennis reached into his coat and pulled out a small journal-looking book. "I wrote down everything that happened. I kept everything in order. I made sure to keep the details strong and I put time stamps on the pages to keep it all in order. This…" Dennis pushed the journal closer to the Commander. "This is the story of Bermuda."

"What are you suggesting?"

"I think we should publish it, and let the people read the story for themselves."

"What's the difference? Wouldn't it look bad if we just tell the court that they have to read a book if they want any information from us?"

"Maybe a little, but there is a different feeling that books give you. After reading this there is no way someone wouldn't believe it. It's a primary source."

"Hm." The Commander cleared his throat. "Well, what do the rest of you think?"

"I agree with Dennis of course." Amber smiled and put her hand on his arm.

"I think it is a good idea." A lady dressed in a brown jacket with long dark brown hair and glasses spoke. "I think it would be a good way for the public to connect with our FBI station rather than feeling such a distinctive gap."

The other agents in the room all nodded.

"…So you're all in agreement that letting the public read a published journal documenting the events that went down in Bermuda would be the best way to go about this? And what about the court? We can't have the judge read an entire book." Commander Layton questioned.

"We can publish the journal for the public, but during our court hearing we can present pieces of information from the journal ourselves. We can read out the important parts that are necessary for the judge to hear." Dennis suggested.

"I think that would be great. The judge should definitely believe it if we tell them that Lieutenant Fischer documented it all himself directly as the events happened." The lady in glasses said again.

"Well, Alrighty then," the Commander began, "looks like we are publishing Bermuda!"

5:00 PM

"Mom you can't do this to me! I *need* to go, this is insanely important!"

"Yeah well guess what, so is my job. And your little sister can't stay home alone all night." Hyon said while stuffing some clothes into a tightly packed suitcase.

"You can just take a sick day!"

"Mi Cha, listen to me…the reason we moved here is because this job is a great opportunity for us. I can't take a sick day until I am fully secured into this job position."

"Why couldn't we stay in Korea with your dance studio?"

"…That was only half of our income. The other half came from your father. Since he left, I…I unfortunately couldn't support us by myself with that job. I tried, I really did, but it just wasn't enough. I'm sorry, I wish I could still do it, but it's simply not enough. This is hard for me too, but this job could get us over 100 thousand a year."

"…Whatever. I'm losing out on a great opportunity too, you know." Mi Cha turned around and marched up the stairs to her bedroom on the upper floor. Hyon let out a small breath of air and wiped her face with the palm of her hands. She dropped the last piece of clothing into the suitcase and zipped it shut. She grabbed her tan blazer jacket from the edge of the bed and pulled it on over her white blouse and matching black pencil skirt. She pulled the suitcase down from the bed onto the floor and extended the telescoping handle. She shut the light and closed the bedroom door as she pulled the suitcase along into the living room. A young child ran out from the kitchen over to Hyon; she was a 6 year old girl.

"Hey you." Hyon said to the little girl. "I'll just be gone for the one night. Mi Cha unnie will take care of you while I'm gone, okay."

"Okay mommy. Annyeong!"

"Haha, Annyeong Nari." Hyon said while she made her way to the door. "Mi Cha, I'm leaving now!" She yelled up the staircase. "Goodbye sweetie!"

Hyon opened the front door to see a young woman standing at the porch. She was short, with dark hair and dressed casually in jeans and flats.

"Oh my, Sarah, what are you doing here?"

"I just got a call from my boss saying that one of the other workers will be able to cover my shift, so I'm free tonight to babysit for you. I'm sorry for the late change of plans." The woman said.

"…Oh, to babysit…" Hyon turned her head back inside the house and gazed at the stairs, then turned back to the woman. "That's great, I'm glad you're free. Mi Cha has been begging me to let her go out with some boy, but I told her she would have to stay and watch her sister. But if you could do it that then would be great! I know Mi Cha would be really happy."

"Yeah, no problem. I don't have anything else to do tonight now. I'm excited to see the girls again anyway!"

"Thank you Sarah! You're a life saver. So how much do you want for this?" Hyon tilted her suitcase vertically so that it would stand up. She began to reach into her purse to grab some money.

"Oh, don't worry about it now. Really, it's fine."

"Oh, alright. Let me just go tell Nari that you'll be watching her instead. Here, please come in." Hyon tugged her suitcase over the lip of the doorframe and back into the house. With her other hand she held the door open for Sarah. "Hey sweetie, look, Sarah is back! She will be watching you for tonight okay?" Hyon spoke to Nari, her 6 year old daughter.

"Hi Sarah!" Nari ran up and hugged her babysitter, Sarah, around the legs.

"Mi Cha has somewhere to go this evening too…hey Mi Cha!" Hyon called up the stairs to Mi Cha and she came walking down the steps and stopped about halfway down. "Hey honey, Sarah is back to babysit. She'll be able to stay to watch Nari, so you can go out with your boyfriend tonight."

"Oh my god, thank you!" Mi Cha thanked Sarah then made her way back upstairs to get ready."

Hyon grabbed the handle of her suitcase once again and rested her other hand on the door handle.

"Thank you again Sarah. You just have to stay until Mi Cha gets back, then they should be fine on their own for the rest of the night. I'll be back in the morning. Nari, you behave yourself for Sarah, you hear?"

"Ah, don't worry. They always behave." Sarah smiled at Hyon then turned to Nari. "We'll have a great time tonight, don't worry."

Hyon pulled open the door. The suitcase slid over the metal and scraped against the door as it tried to shut itself.

"Annyeong mommy!"

6:00 PM

"What do you mean he is gone from his cell?" Dennis talked with Officer Braidy as she led him through the halls of the prison up to the 6th floor. A group of four other officers were crowded around a cell at the end of the hall.

"This is how we found it. It's closed AND locked. There is no sign of forced entry or any sort of breakage at all. And as you can see, no Zando."

"Zando…that name sounds familiar to me. Which one of you was the officer on duty to watch over this floor?" Dennis questioned the four officers.

"None of us sir." Officer Philips spoke up. "It was supposed to be Officer Browden, but he didn't show up for duty today."

"Is he the only one with a key to this cell?"

"No sir. The four of us plus Browden and Miss Braidy all have access to the keys for all of the cells."

"Hm, okay. Well, what I see here is that we must have a mole. Someone let Zando out on purpose, hence the no evidence of a breakout. And if he was let out *today* then that would eliminate Officer Browden from the suspect list since he wasn't here. So what I will do when I get back to headquarters tomorrow is start a search party to find Zando. But first, I'm curious to see the security camera footage, if you don't mind."

"Sure thing. Follow me." Officer Braidy started to lead Dennis back to the elevator. They walked down the hallway full of cells as one prisoner jumped up flush against the cold steel bars. He had long, dirty hair and a rough unshaven beard.

"It's the Vaska's. The Vaska tribe! They are preparing for the lord to rise again! They're going to resurrect their lord!" The prisoner yelled.

"…The Vaskas?" Dennis repeated.

"…Don't mind him." Officer Braidy spoke to Dennis. "He is one of our mental care patients." She tapped on the *down* button with her pointer finger. The elevator dinged as the doors pealed apart. Dennis and Braidy hopped inside and descended down to the surveillance room.

The car sped down the highway. The awaiting sunset floated on the horizon line like a small sphere of glowing red energy. The surrounding clouds appeared pink in the darkening skies. All was quiet. The sounds of the speeding vehicles were all that was heard.

Inside the small red Hyundai coupe came voices from the radio. Commercials played as Hyun drove calmly with her hands in a fixed position on the wheel. The neon green lights behind it displayed her speed and the amount of gas in the tank. The bar for gas was low and flashed red. Hyon pulled the car off onto the next exit leading to the nearest rest stop. She pulled up to an empty pump and parked the car. She got out and pressed the button for regular gas and stuck the nozzle into the tank on the back of the car. She let it fill to the max then replaced the nozzle in its compartment before she made her way inside and up to the front counter to pay.

"Full tank on number four." Hyon said to the cashier.

She set her purse down on the counter and began digging through it to find her money. There was a TV on the wall just above the man's head. The banner along the bottom of the screen read *Breaking News.* Hyon handed the man her money and gazed up at the television screen as he logged some numbers into the register.

"We have breaking news of an escaped prisoner from the Seattle county jail. He is a tall, broad shouldered black African male and goes by the name of Zando. Police say he is extremely dangerous and could possibly be armed. If you see this man please report to the police immediately. The FBI have begun a search of their own in collaboration with the local police. Until they find him, stay safe. This has been Samantha Paladino with your breaking news."

"Oh wow, did you hear that?"

"Yeah, sure did. I can't believe it. How can someone just break out like that? I bet somebody let him out." The cashier spoke.

"Could be." Hyon agreed. "Well, have a good night."

"Thanks, you as well. Stay safe. If you have kids, keep them safe too."

"I will.

7:00 PM

Mi Cha and her boyfriend Anthony walked up to the ticket booth. Mi Cha was wearing white skinny jeans with a black sleeveless top that cut off just above her belly button. She wore matching black heeled sandals on her feet. Her hair was a very light brown and was pulled to fall over the left side of her face. Anthony wore light grey colored jeans with a thin black cardigan sweater. His dark hair was gelled up and pulled over to the side. They were both 17 years old.

"Two tickets to *Raven's Eye* please." Anthony spoke to the lady running the stand.

"Umm…it's rated R. I'm not supposed to let you guys into it unless you're 18."

"Well…if we promise that our parents won't sue the theatre for showing their teenage kids some slight nudity and a few swear words, then can we get in?"

"I'm really not allowed to and I don't want to lose my job over something like that."

"…Okay fine. We'll take two tickets to the *Blue's Clues* remake movie then."

Anthony paid for both his and Mi Cha's tickets then bought a soda and some popcorn from the concession stand. They both made their way to the man collecting tickets on the left wing of the theatre.

"…Takin' your girl to go see Blue's Clues eh?" The man smiled as he tore the top portion of the tickets off. "I know what you're doing…don't worry though, I won't say anything. Enjoy your date."

"Thank you." Anthony said as he and Mi Cha walked down to the end of the hall.

"Wait, so are we actually going to see *Raven's Eye*?" Mi Cha questioned.

"I mean, *Blue's Clues* is always a good option, but *Raven's Eye* looks pretty awesome." Anthony smiled and planted a kiss on Mi Cha's cheek. "Your eyes are so pretty."

"Yeah, you like Asian eyes don't you?"

"I do. They are pretty hot." Anthony said.

"That's not the only thing that's hot on me." Mi Cha laughed.

"Very true, very true."

"Yeah. Sooo, are we going to go watch this movie or are you just going to stand here and compliment me all night?" Mi Cha shifted her weight onto her right leg and crossed her arms in front of her stomach.

"I mean, whatever you want. Either option is fine with me."

"Hmm…how about movie now and then you can complement me as much as you want to afterwards."

Anthony smiled and followed Mi Cha to the last door at the end of the hall. He held it open as she walked into the dark theatre room.

7:30 PM

"Right there!" Dennis pointed at the computer screen. "Did you see that? Play that back."

Officer Braidy sat at the desk with her fingers on the keyboard playing the surveillance tapes for Dennis. The scene on the camera showed the end of the hall with a view of the last four cells. Braidy rewound the clip to see Zando sitting at the edge of his bed inside his cell. The clip played for a few seconds until Zando suddenly disappeared.

"Look at that. He just vanishes. Play it back really slowly."

Braidy rewound the tape again and slowed it down so that it was now only frame by frame. She clicked through each frame until the image came to a fuzzy black and white blur. The next frame after, Zando was gone.

"There it is." Officer Braidy said as she went back to the fuzzy screen. "What do you suppose it could be?"

"It looks to me like the video was cropped. Whoever let Zando out also must have also cut out the video footage of themselves doing it so that nobody could know who it was."

"So you're saying that the culprit is definitely one of us officers?"

"I mean, it's always possible somebody could have broken in, but I have a strong feeling that somebody here is responsible. If there were no holes or any broken bars in his cell then that would eliminate the possibility of him

escaping on his own. I'm also sure that somebody from the outside wouldn't be able to walk in here in the middle of the day and gain access to the 6th floor to break somebody out without getting caught. So, I'm sorry to say this, but it's almost certain that somebody working here is a mole; they either let Zando out themselves or simply turned a blind eye and had somebody else do it."

"I have no idea who it could be. I've always trusted my coworkers, I can't see why something like this would happen." Braidy said as she turned around in her chair to face Dennis.

"Are you the officer in charge here?"

"Yes, why?"

"For the time being I want you to take away the other officers' keys. I don't want anybody having access to any of these rooms or other cells besides you. If some of them need the keys for something make sure you go with them and keep an eye out. If we can make sure only one person—you—has the keys, then should make our job much easier if something else should happen."

"Yes of course. I'll go collect everybody's keys right now." Officer Braidy stood up and began to walk out from the surveillance room with Dennis.

"Email me that surveillance video too. I'll have my team analyze it a little better."

"Sure thing Lieutenant Fischer."

8:00 PM

Dennis pulled his car up into the driveway. The house was large and modern looking. It had two floors with large, glass picture windows on the front wall. The walls were made of clean looking stone. Neatly trimmed hedges and colorful flowers decorated the front yard. The grass was cut short with an oval shaped water fountain pond in the middle of the lawn. Dennis parked his black Porsche and walked up the lighted cobblestone sidewalk to the front door. With the turn of a key, he was inside.

A large marble staircase greeted him in the foyer upon entry. The floors were a light tan marble. A rectangular area rug with an abstract pattern covered the center of the cold marble. There were two large openings on each side wall leading to different rooms and to the left of the stairs, a hallway leading forward. Dennis made his way through the left opening where Amber stood at the stove cooking something in a pan. She wore black lounge shorts with a thin white tank top.

"There's my girl." Dennis said as he walked over to her and hugged her from behind. "What are you making?"

"I found this really cool recipe for these spicy chicken cutlets fried in wine and butter. I know you usually don't like spicy foods but this is a good kind of spicy. It's a soft and smooth tang, not like obnoxiously tangy or anything."

"Mm, sounds delicious. You know what else is soft and smooth?"

"Haha, I think I do know. But come on, let's eat first."

Amber grabbed two plates from the cabinet and set them in front of two chairs at the table. The kitchen had the same marble floor with granite counter tops. The cabinets were a dark cherry wood as well as the legs of the table in the center of the room. The refrigerator and washing machine were both a shiny silver.

Dennis grabbed two glasses from the cupboard and held them under the water dispenser on the door of the fridge. Amber set two chicken cutlets on each plate followed by some rice mixed with peppers and onions.

"So were you able to find out anything new about that escaped prisoner?" Amber asked upon seating.

"I looked at the surveillance tapes and someone had cropped out a piece of it. You can see Zando in his cell one minute and then he suddenly just disappears. Now, I know we've seen some crazy stuff you and I, but one thing I do not believe in is ghosts. So, that means that of those officers let Zando out purposely and edited out the surveillance footage as a cover up."

"Want me to start running background checks on each of the officers?"

"Yes, that would be good. If we can find out *who* let Zando out, then we can find where he is, and then we can catch him and put them both in jail."

"That is unless they mysteriously vanish from their cells too." Amber joked.

They both sat for ten more minutes finishing their meals and discussing the case. Amber swallowed the last bite of her chicken then brought her plate back up to the sink.

"Okay. I'll go get those background checks started." Amber headed towards the hallway but Dennis stood up and blocked her.

"Not so fast. Last time I checked computers are not soft and smooth…I was promised to get something soft and smooth after dinner."

"Soft and smooth huh?" Follow me." Amber grabbed Dennis's hand and pulled him along down the hallway, up the stairs, and to the opened bedroom door at the end. She led him inside and pushed him down onto the bed.

The room was large. A king sized bed was centered along the front wall. Large, closet doors plated with mirrors covered the left wall. The right wall had a large glass window looking out onto an outdoor patio with a swimming pool on the ground level below. There was a large, flat screen TV on the wall opposite the bed and an artificial palm tree in the corner. The floor was hardwood with a large, cream colored area rug which matched the bed comforter. The pillows were neatly decorated and set evenly at the head of the bed. When Dennis fell onto the mattress, the front two pillows tipped over.

Amber slid open the closet door and bent down to grab something. She lifted herself and turned back around to face Dennis.

"Happy early Easter." She spoke as a large, stuffed bunny rabbit sat in her arms. "It's soft and smooth, just the way you like it."

"Oh haha, that's very funny." Dennis stood up and grabbed the bunny. He stared at its black glossy eyes and large dangly pink ears. "Cute." He said before he tossed it aside onto the bed and wrapped his arms around Amber's waist.

"Now let me give you *my* Easter gift."

"Oh yeah, and what does this gift entail?"

"Let me show you." Dennis turned Amber around and walked her back to the edge of the bed. As her legs touched the wooden frame she sat down and lay flat on her back against the surface. Dennis climbed on top of her on his knees and kissed her neck, then moved to her lips. His right hand reached down to her waist and underneath her shirt. He moved his hand up, and slid it across her stomach and up to her chest. He pulled at her shirt with both hands until it came up, over her head and off of her arms.

Amber smiled and sat up. "This isn't really an Easter-themed gift I see." She said.

"Well, Easter isn't for one more week. Consider this a spur of the moment gift."

Amber smiled again and reached her hands behind her back and unhooked her bra. Dennis pulled his shirt off and wrestled Amber onto her stomach. He grabbed her shorts by the elastic and pulled them down off of her legs. Amber flipped around onto her back again as she kissed Dennis.

"Well, you were right. This *is* a better gift than that stuffed bunny." Amber smiled as she reached down and unbuckled Dennis' pants.

10:00 PM

The sound of the front door creaking open from downstairs pulled Sarah away from washing her face in the bathroom sink.

"Nari, is that you?" Sarah quickly shut off the water and pulled a towel to her face. She trotted down the stairs while she dabbed her face dry. She was halfway down the steps when she felt the sudden cool breeze brush up against her skin. The front door was wide open, and was swaying back and forth with the breeze. She dropped the towel over the top edge of the couch and went over to close it.

"Nari? Are you down here?" Sarah clicked the door shut and turned for the kitchen. The sound of glass and ice clanging together filled her ears as she stepped inside. Nari was standing in her pajamas at the refrigerator placing ice cubes into a tall glass of water.

"There you are. Are you getting ready for bed, it's getting late?"

"I'm getting water first." Nari shut the door and held the glass carefully between her hands. The water was filled right to the top.

"Make sure you brush your teeth before sleeping. And be careful with that water walking up the stairs. Don't make any messes."

"I won't spill any. Can you come tuck me in?" Nari said and walked back through the living room to get to the stairs.

"Of course, but after you brush."

Once they were both upstairs inside Nari's room, Sarah took the glass of water and placed it onto the small table by Nari's bedside as she went to brush her teeth in the bathroom. Sarah rolled down the blankets and fluffed up the pillows. A soft lamp was turned on, which lighted up the bright colored walls and pile of stuffed animals in the corner of the room, near the closet.

Nari came trotting back into the bedroom and hopped right up onto the bed. She pulled the blanket over her legs and took a long sip of the water.

"Mommy says drinking water before bed is good for you."

"Good girl." Sarah helped pull the blanket over the rest of Nari's body and gave her a soft pat on her head. She clicked the lamp off and headed for the door when she heard Nari sit back up. When she turned around, Nari was pointing a finger at the pile of stuffed animals in the corner.

"What's wrong? You want one of your toys?" Sarah turned the bright light switch back on from the wall and reached down to pick up a toy. She touched the arm of a large rabbit sitting in the middle of the pile.

"You want this one? It's bigger than you, haha."

Nari shook her head no.

"You don't want it?"

"I've never seen that one before, did you get it for me?"

"No, I didn't. Your mother probably did as an early Easter gift."

Nari lowered herself back into a laying position as Sarah shut the lights off once again. She closed the door softly and made her way back downstairs. The television was on and a half empty bottle of Pepsi sat next to a bag of potato chips on the coffee table. Sarah plopped herself down onto the couch and brought the soda to her mouth. It fizzed down her throat until she let out a soft burp. She grabbed the remote control and turned the volume up a few notches. A high pitched scream blasted through the house.

Sarah jolted up when she realized that the scream didn't come from the television. She ran around the couch and up the stairs to the end of the hall where Nari's room sat. She charged inside to see Nari standing on the top of her bed, pointing at the pile of stuffed animals again.

"What's wrong? Are you okay?"

"The bunny." Nari replied.

Sarah turned her gaze to the large yellow rabbit sitting in the pile of toys. Its eyes stared straight at Nari's bed.

"Are you scared of it, huh? It's just a stuffed animal, it can't hurt you."

"Don't leave me alone with it."

"Nari, relax. You need to get to sleep, it's late." Sarah took Nari's arm and sat her back down on the bed. She pulled the blanket over her body again.

"Goodnight Nari. Sleep well." Sarah shut the lights off again and left the room. She made her way back downstairs to the living room where she pulled out her cellphone and dialed Hyon's number.

"Sarah, hey, is everything alright?" Hyon answered the call.

"Everything's fine Ms. Park, I just tucked her into bed now. Although, she seems to be pretty afraid of her new stuffed bunny toy haha."

"What stuffed bunny?"

"The big yellow one. Sitting in the middle of the pile. You know, the one that's like bigger than she is."

"I…don't know what you're talking about. Nari doesn't have any kind of bunny toy."

"What? That can't be."

Another loud, piercing scream blasted through the house as a rumbling sound came from Nari's bedroom. The phone dropped to the floor as Sarah ran to the stairs.

"Sarah?! What's happening? Hello?!"

11:30 PM

"Your eyes are gorgeous, you have amazing hair, you dress very fashionably, you smell nice, umm…you have cute uh, cute boobs, your butt is—

"Haha, what are you doing?" Mi Cha cut Anthony off.

"Well, you said that when we finished the movie I could compliment you all night long."

"True. Looks like it'll have to stop for now though, we're at my house."

Anthony drove the car up into the driveway. He parked it and shut off the headlights.

"Well, I had a great time tonight." He said.

"Yeah, me too. It was a great movie. I can't believe Cynthia got defeated in the end. I hope there will be a Raven's Eye 2 in the future. I would love to see Cynthia come back!"

"Yeah it was really good. But to be honest, Blues Clues would have been just as enjoyable as long as I was watching it with you." Anthony reached one arm over around Mi Cha's shoulders. He moved his head inward and pressed his lips against hers. With his other hand he cupped the side of her face. His head moved in slight motions as he kissed Mi Cha.

"…I think I got some of your lip gloss on my lips."

"Just marking my territory. Never wipe that off now."

"I'm definitely going to wipe it off; that way you will have to keep marking it up." Anthony smiled as he exited the vehicle and walked Mi Cha up to the front door. The overhead lamp above the door was on, casting light onto each of their faces.

"So I'm having an Easter party at my house this Saturday, I would love it if you could come." Anthony proposed.

"Oh, I would love to, but my little sister has this Easter decorating party at her school that day. It's supposed to be a 'family' thing, ya know."

"Ah, that's fine. You can just come to my house later that night then…when everybody else is gone."

Mi Cha dropped her head and bit her lip slightly, then raised it again. "Yeah, okay. That sounds good."

"Alright cool. Well I will see you then, then. Then then? I will see you then…then. Is that correct grammar?"

"Hmm, I have no idea haha."

"Alright, well goodnight baby. Or ah…annyeong gizibe, right?"

"Gizibe means bitch in Korean."

"Oh. Well you're *my* gizibe."

Mi Cha shook her head and laughed as Anthony walked back to his car. She waited until he pulled away and honked before she made her way inside.

She entered into a quiet, still house. Toys and stuffed animals lay scattered around the living room floor. The TV was turned on, but the volume was quiet. It cast a blue light onto the couch and walls. A half bottle of Pepsi sat on the coffee table next to an opened bag of potato chips.

Mi Cha flipped on the light switch to her right, turning on the ceiling lamp. "Nari! Sarah!" She called out after dropping her bag and coat onto the arm of the couch.

She made her way to the kitchen and saw the snack closet left open. The cupboard door for the glasses was half open. The drawer to the silverware was not shut completely.

"Nari!" Mi Cha called again.

As she came back into the living room she saw Sarah's cell phone face down on the floor by the side of the couch. She bent down and turned it over—last call was made to *Hyon Park*.

Mi Cha made her way up the stairs, barging into each room that she passed by. The bathroom, her room, her mom's room; each one gave the same quiet, empty vibe. Finally she made her way to Nari's room at the end of the hallway. Upon turning on the lights, Mi Cha noticed a small lump hiding underneath the pink bed comforter. It had a round head shape and a curved body silhouette.

"Nari, are you sleeping?" Mi Cha approached the side of the bed and kneeled down. She grabbed hold of the top corner of the comforter and pulled it down.

Mi Cha flinched back as she was greeted with large pink eyes, long flappy ears, a pink snout with white whiskers, small thin arms, a yellow furry body with the letter **A** printed in its stomach, and a large puffy cotton tail. Mi Cha pulled the small stuffed rabbit away and rummaged through the sheets until she realized that the bunny was the only occupant in the bed.

She lifted her eyes to the corner of the room where the rug was stained dark red. She lifted herself from her kneeling position as the body slowly came into view. First the arms, then the torso, then the head. Mi Cha covered her mouth in a scream as she watched the body lay motionless in a puddle of blood. A large wound was ripped in the chest—it was Sarah.

CHAPTER 2

March 18th 2018

12:05 AM

"What happened?" Amber asked after Dennis hung up the phone.

"We have to go. A girl called in to the station saying her little sister is missing and babysitter has been murdered. She is all alone in the house."

Dennis sat at the edge of the bed putting on his black pants. Amber pushed back the covers and swung her feet over to the floor. She grabbed a pair of dark jeans and a white blouse from the dresser. Dennis finished tying his shoe laces and pulled his black coat over his button down shirt. Amber slipped on a pair of black heels and pulled on her waistcoat. They each grabbed their badges from the small table by the bedroom door and hooked them onto their jackets.

Dennis and Amber made their way outside into the cool, nighttime breeze. They hopped inside the black SUV—the blue and red lights on the dashboard lit up in a neon glow. The engine roared loudly in the silent streets. Dennis radioed in to base.

"This is Fischer. Where was that girl's location?"

"The house is on 1126 Brigham Street."

"Thank you Commander." Dennis locked the radio speaker back into place and drove off down the road.

Mi Cha sat at the edge of the couch in front of the half empty bottle of Pepsi. The TV was still on, but it was muted. Mi Cha's white cell phone sat clasped in between her hands as her legs shook up and down in nervousness. She felt sick to even stay inside the house knowing that Sarah's dead body was lying upstairs. She couldn't leave and wait anywhere else though because she was also too afraid for that. Instead, she sat as far on the edge of the couch as she could and watched outside through the window. She waited nervously as her body shook and eyes filled with tears.

As bright headlights pierced through the thin window curtains, Mi Cha jumped up and watched as Dennis and Amber exited their vehicle and walked up to the front door.

"Hello, I am Agent Berns." Amber smiled and held out her hand as Mi Cha opened the door before she had time to knock or ring the doorbell. "What is your name?"

"Mi Cha."

"Well Mi Cha, is there anybody else in the house right now?" Dennis questioned as he came up to the door a few seconds after.

"No, my mom is away on a business trip for the night."

"Okay, well, let's have you take a seat here and tell us what happened." Dennis guided Mi Cha over to take a

seat on the couch. Amber sat down next to her while Dennis continued to stand. "Firstly, how old are you?"

"17."

"Ok. So what is the story?" Dennis questioned.

"My mom went away for the night on a business trip, and I was out at the movies with my boyfriend, so my little sister Nari stayed home. When I came back, about 20 minutes ago, she was gone. I saw a lump in her comforter and thought she was in there but when I pulled them back it was just a stuffed rabbit." Mi Cha explained as she tried to fight back tears.

"Was anybody else in the house with her? Your sister."

"Yes. There was our babysitter Sarah." Mi Cha began to sob. "But…but when I looked up from Nari bed I saw her body on the floor in the corner."

"Oh my." Amber said softly. "And there was nobody else in the house except for your sister Nari and Sarah?"

Mi Cha shook her head then moved her hand to her eyes as she began to cry some more.

"Okay. It's going to be okay honey, don't cry." Amber put her hand around Mi Cha shoulder's and gave her a little rub.

"Can we go see the room?" Dennis asked.

"Yeah." Mi Cha tried to wipe her face dry. Her legs shook as she stood up to lead Dennis and Amber up the stairs to Nari's room at the end of the hall. The bed

comforter was bunched up in a pile at the foot of the bed and the stuffed bunny lay on its side on the floor. "Here's the bunny." Mi Cha said while picking it up and handing it to Dennis. "It isn't ours."

"…So you're saying that someone else, not Nari nor Sarah, must have left this here under the covers?"

Mi Cha raised her shoulders in a shrug.

"Probably the person who killed Sarah left this here." Dennis said as he stepped over slowly to the corner of the room and peered down at Sarah's body. He shook his head in sickness at the large open gash in the middle of her stomach where blood was continuously pouring from. "Okay, let's not stay in here." He said as he stepped back over to the middle of the room. "Why don't you come with me Mi Cha and give me some more information about everything that happened so I can document it in a file for investigation. Amber, why don't you go call in to the station to have them come pick up the body. And contact this girl's mother to let her know what's going on."

"Of course." Amber replied as she pulled out her cellphone and dialed the number to the FBI station. Dennis led Mi Cha out of the bedroom and back downstairs to the living room.

"Hi, this is Agent Berns. Lieutenant Fischer and I are here at the Park's house. We need somebody to come and pick up the body. Also, can you direct me to Hyon Park's phone please?"

"They are on their way right now. And of course, one second let me just look up her phone information." The receptionist on the phone replied.

"Hello." Hyon answered her cell phone from a hotel room. The room had a queen bed, TV, bathroom, and a large glass window looking out onto the nighttime city.

"Hi Ms. Park, this is Agent Berns of the FBI. We were called to your house by your daughter Mi Cha. She said she came home and found her little sister, Nari, missing from bed, and that her babysitter was found dead."

"What?! What do you mean?"

"…Your youngest daughter is missing. Sarah, your babysitter, we also believe was murdered based on the type of wound she has on her stomach. Mi Cha is safe with us right now so you don't need to panic, but I can imagine this isn't easy information for you to take in. For your daughter Nari, we are going to conduct an official investigation to try to find her. We believe that somebody must have broken in and kidnapped her, after killing Sarah."

"Oh my god! Wha, what do I do? I'm all the way here in Spokane. There's no way I could make it back home until morning." Hyon spoke with a shaky voice. "Is…is Mi Cha safe? Where is she?"

"Mi Cha is perfectly okay, she's just talking with my partner Lieutenant Fischer downstairs."

"Oh, oh my god. I…What am I going to do? What do I do?"

"Just stay calm Ms. Park. If you can't make it back here until morning then Dennis and I would be willing to look after Mi Cha for you."

"Oh, oh yes, please. Don't let her go anywhere alone. I, I'll start heading home right now!"

"Okay, we'll take Mi Cha back to our house for the night just to be sure that nobody tries to come back here."

"Where do you think Nari is? Is she going to be okay? Will you be able to find her?" Hyon spoke frantically.

"…Right now we have no details on anything. What I predict, based on my experience, is that she *is* still alive. If the kidnapper wanted her dead, he would have done it already and left her body in the house with Sarah's. So, I believe that she *is* alive and I promise you that we will do our best to find her. Mi Cha will be safe with us so you have nothing to worry about. Drive safe and just try to remain calm okay? That's the best thing that you can do."

"…Yeah, I'll try to. I'll be alright. Thank you so much for calling me ma'am. I just feel so…so helpless. I should have been there to protect my children." Hyon began to cry.

"It's okay Ms. Park, don't blame yourself. There's no telling what could've happened even if you were there. Right now, just relax and come back home. We will handle the rest from here on."

"I'll try Ms. Berns...my daughter though. I can't…I can't believe somebody would kidnap her. But thank you for watching Mi Cha for the night. I'll be back first thing tomorrow morning."

"No problem Ms. Park, it's our job to protect. You take care now. Goodbye."

Amber put her phone back into her coat pocket and headed out the bedroom door as her foot kicked the side of the stuffed rabbit. It rolled over onto its back, revealing the yellow and white colored stomach with the letter **A** on it. Amber bent down and picked it up. She brought it with her downstairs to the living room.

"Hey Dennis, this bunny has the letter 'A' imprinted on its stomach. Do you think it could mean anything?"

"Hm, interesting. Does the letter 'A' have any sort of significance to you or your family Mi Cha?"

"…I…I don't see any connection. Unless A stands for Asian." Mi Cha let out a boiled down, shaky laugh. Amber smiled back.

"Well…it is a yellow bunny." Dennis added.

"…You're not really suggesting that are you?" Amber questioned. "You're saying that the kidnapper purposely targeted Nari because she is Asian?" She walked over and set the bunny down on the coffee table in front of the couch.

"I mean, it could be. It *very* well could be."

"Did you tell Dennis everything he needed to know?" Amber asked Mi Cha.

"Yes she did. I wrote down everything she could give me. So, I think we're good for tonight." Dennis closed his notepad and capped his pen.

"Okay. Mi Cha, your mom wants you to come stay with us tonight to keep you safe, okay? Why don't you go grab some extra clothes and sleepwear and we'll head over there now."

Dennis tucked his notepad into his inner coat pocket as Mi Cha headed up the stairs to grab some clothes from her bedroom.

"…What do you think the kidnapper wants with Nari?" Amber whispered.

"I don't know. It doesn't make sense. He doesn't want to kill her. Not yet at least. And if his motive is rape then you would think he would want to find somebody a little older. I mean Nari is only 6 years old."

"We *need* to find her."

"We will find her. Don't worry. Let's take this bunny with us for evidence."

Mi Cha descended the staircase with a small bag of clothes in her right hand and her cell phone clung in her left. Amber led her outside to the SUV that was parked in the driveway. Mi Cha climbed up into the backseat as Dennis and Amber hopped in the front.

Dennis backed up and pulled off down the road. The night was clear and calm. Mi Cha rolled down her window in the back to feel the slight breeze brush against her face. The scent of moist air and blooming pollen filled the vehicle. The car tires sped against the slick road and splashed through the small puddles.

"How are you holding up?" Amber reached her head over the side of her car seat to face Mi Cha.

"I'm okay. I'm just extremely scared. I want to believe she will be okay, but it just worries me not knowing what kind of danger she could be in."

"I know how you feel." Dennis chimed in. "I've been in a similar situation before with my former Lieutenant. Lieutenant Vira was her name—Martha Vira. She sacrificed herself to save Amber and I. She stayed inside a burning building to find the bad guy just so we could escape safely. It was when we were in Bermuda…"

Dennis pulled the car up the lighted driveway and parked it inside the garage. Amber led Mi Cha inside through the doorway to the kitchen and clicked the light switch on, filling the darkness of the rooms with bright light.

"Oh wow, so are you guys like really rich?" Mi Cha walked forward into the marble encrusted entry hall and staircase.

"Maybe not. Maybe we just spent all of our money on this house." Amber said then smiled back at Dennis. "Feel free to use whatever you want to. Any food in the kitchen you can have, any drink. And there is a guest bedroom upstairs—make yourself at home."

"Thank you. I'll probably just go to sleep now. It's late and I'm too nervous to eat or drink anything."

"Ok, we're going to. Goodnight. I'll make breakfast for us all in the morning, how does that sound?" Amber smiled and waved goodnight to Mi Cha as she headed up the stairs to the guest bedroom.

The Next Morning

Mi Cha opened her eyes to a dim room. The sun was just beginning to filter inside through the curtains on each side of the bed. A soft breeze coming through the windows flitted the thin fabric. Mi Cha pushed the comforter to the side and swung her feet over the edge of the bed. She felt the soft press of the warm carpet on her toes. The alarm clock on the nearby night table read *9:45.* Mi Cha opened the bedroom door to a rectangular block of white light. The brightness from the outside hallway blinded her for a few seconds until her eyes adjusted. She made her way down the cold, marble staircase to the entry hall below.

The fresh smell of butter, eggs, and oranges suddenly crept its way up into her nostrils. Through the archway on the left wall, Mi Cha could see Amber at the stove with a spatula in her hand and a frying pan on the burner, with a plate of French toast next to it. Dennis was standing over the table pouring three glasses of orange juice. The scents grew stronger as Mi Cha approached the kitchen table.

"Good morning Mi Cha!" Amber said while placing the last three French toasts onto the platter. She carried it over to the table and set it down right in front of an empty chair. "Have as much as you would like."

"Thank you, it looks delicious." Mi Cha grabbed the back of the chair and pulled it out to sit down. She picked up two pieces of French toast from the platter and placed them onto her own plate. She began to cut the slices into smaller pieces before pouring the syrup on.

Dennis sat down with a newspaper, sipping his orange juice. A ring from the doorbell prevented Amber from doing the same; she hurried over to the front door and opened it.

"Agent Berns, hello. I'm Hyon Park. Mi Cha's mother." Hyon stood at the doorway dressed in a formal work suit. Her hair was up in a neat bun and her makeup was untampered.

"Yes, please come in. She's just eating breakfast now."

Amber led Hyon to the kitchen. When she saw her daughter she quickly ran to her and wrapped her arms around her shoulders.

"Mi Cha honey, are you okay? I'm so sorry I couldn't get here sooner!"

"I'm okay. Dennis and Amber showed up to the house in less than ten minutes after I called."

"Oh I'm so relieved to hear that. I'm so glad you're okay…So do you guys have any more information or leads yet?" Hyon asked cautiously.

"…Um, no. Nothing yet. But there is a search party on the lookout for your daughter Nari and we are running background checks on Sarah to see if she would have any possible enemies." Amber took a seat next to Dennis on the opposite side of Mi Cha and Hyon.

"…Right." Hyon replied.

"I can assure you we will do the best that we can. Your case is in good hands." Dennis responded.

"Yeah, why don't you eat a little? You probably haven't eaten anything your whole drive here."

"Okay, you're right. I should try to relax." Hyon let out a long breath of air and took a seat next to her daughter.

"Here, let me get you a plate."

"Tyreese, there you are! Where the hell have you been the past few days?" Officer Braidy sat up in her chair as Tyreese Browden walked through the office doors.

He was dark skinned with closely shaved hair and a small scar on his forehead. He had a large nose, big eyes, and was dressed in his blue police uniform.

"…One of my close relatives is sick. I had to do what I could to help him…"

"Okay, well you are supposed to call in and let me know you won't be working then. You know the rules….So did you hear the news?"

"What news?" Tyreese made his way to the coffee table to pour a cup.

"The news that Zando broke out…someone let him out."

"Do we know who it was?"

"No. Not yet. Agent Fischer of the FBI told me to keep hold on all of the keys until we find out who it was—to make sure they don't try anything else sneaky."

"Well it sure as hell ain't me. I wasn't even here that day."

The small black phone that was mounted on the wall began to ring. Officer Braidy set aside her newspaper to go answer it.

"Seattle Police Department, Officer Braidy speaking."

"Please, you have to help me! My, my son is missing. He is only 4 years old! Please, you've got to find him—

"Okay, okay ma'am please calm down. Tell me your address and I'll send someone over."

"Yes, it's uh, 8691 Balik Road."

"Okay got it; just stay where you are and relax okay." Officer Braidy clicked the phone back onto the mount then pulled it back off, up to her ear.

"Hello Agent Fischer, this is Officer Braidy. I just got a call of another child disappearance—a 4 year old boy. I have no idea if it's connected in any way to the Park family, but it very well could be. The address is 8691 Balik Road. I'm headed over there now."

"Okay, this is big news! I'll head over there right away." Dennis ended the call and stood up from the kitchen table. He gulped down the remainder of the orange juice in his glass and set it on the counter near the sink.

"…What is it?" Amber questioned.

"…Another child disappearance—a 4 year old boy. It could very possibly be connected somehow to Nari. You could stay here though if you want, Officer Braidy will be meeting me there."

"Oh my!" Hyon gasped. "How can someone be so evil?!"

"If the same man that kidnapped Nari also kidnapped this boy then this should make finding him a lot easier." Dennis grabbed a coat from the closet next the door near the garage and pulled it over his white t shirt. "I'll let you know what I can find."

When Dennis pulled up to the house, a black and white police car was already parked in the driveway. He parked his own SUV on the side of the road and made his way up to the front door. Inside, Officer Braidy was sitting, talking with the mother, as a couple of other officers stood against the wall. The mother sat with tears in her eyes while holding a crumbled up tissue in between her hands.

"What's the story for far?" Dennis asked as he approached the two officers against the wall.

"They are a European family who moved here a few years ago. She says she tucked her son into bed at night and then went to sleep herself. While she was sleeping she thought she heard a noise but didn't think anything of it. When she woke up this morning and checked the son's bedroom, he wasn't there…She also found this laying in her son's bed." One of the officers reached under the coffee table and produced a stuffed rabbit with white fur and the letter **E** sewn onto its stomach.

Dennis nodded his head. "…Okay, it's the same scenario as the Parks; just as I thought. I want both of these rabbits tested for fingerprints, hairs, anything we can find. This kidnapper is clearly planning to strike again, I don't suspect he will stop at two. Send an alert out telling everybody to stay protective if they have small children and don't leave them alone for long."

"You sure about that? We don't want people to panic. There's nothing to say that he will definitely kidnap another." The other officer spoke.

"He's leaving stuffed rabbits to taunt us, don't you see? When they do that, they think that they can outsmart us. And if they think they can outsmart us, then they are much more likely to keep it up. We don't have to scare parents with the alert, just warn them. I want to catch this guy before any other child is kidnapped."

12:00 PM

"Today was supposed to be Nari's Easter decorating day at her school." Hyon sat on the living room couch next to Mi Cha. Bright daylight flustered inside through the thin, transparent curtains. A springtime breeze pushed through the small window opening. "Do you think we should still go? To help out the other kids with the decorating and their crafts and stuff?"

"I…I don't know. You think that would be a good idea?" Mi Cha replied.

"I think we should get out of this house for the day. I can't just sit here and—and just wait for the phone to ring with more information. Every second that goes by I can't stop thinking about Nari. Maybe if we go to the school it'll relax me a little bit more and maybe ease my mind a little bit."

"…Yeah, it might. We can go. Nari was so excited about it, she would want us to go and make some crafts for her."

"And we'll save her some candy and macaroni art pieces and give them to her when she comes back. We'll make her feel really nice when she come back, you know?"

Mi Cha smiled and nodded and headed up the stairs. "I'll go get dressed."

Mi Cha and Hyon rounded the side of wall to the backyard of the school. The sun was high in the sky, providing for a bright, warm day. Long, wooden tables were set up in the grass, covered with boxes and containers of art supplies—colorful crayons, markers, glitters, safety scissors, foam paper, googly eyes, plastic eggs, and wicker baskets. Another table was cluttered with sodas, juices, chips, cookies, and candy. Children scurried from the large playground set, to the snack tables, and back again. They slid down the big red slide, burrowed through the green plastic tubes, and clung for dear life on the monkey bars in fear of some unknown danger lurking below.

Parents sat at the craft table with their children, assisting them with their masterpieces. Mi Cha brushed off a pile of spilled black glitter with her hand from the bench in front of her and took a seat. Hyon sat on the opposite side, facing Mi Cha. The doors to the school were wide open, allowing the children to run inside and out. Some of them ran inside and taped their pieces of artwork to the walls, others decorated the floors of the school with pink, artificial grass. Teachers stood on ladders pinning colorful streamers to the ceilings.

A little boy was inside the school hanging up a painting he had made of a bunny rabbit. The hallway was empty and dark except for the filtered sunlight. A small piece of wrapped up candy was sitting by itself on the floor just a bit further down the hall. The boy went to grab the candy when he noticed another piece just a few feet ahead; there was a small trail of candies leading down the hallway and around the corner. There was nothing except complete darkness at the end of the trail. The boy followed the trail, picking up each piece of candy one by one from the floor and into his pocket.

Mi Cha was gluing a pair of large googly eyes onto a piece of foam that was cut into the shape of a rabbit head. She stuck the plastic eyes onto the spot she glued and pressed them down tightly for a few minutes. Hyon was sitting across from her and was talking to the mother of one of Nari's friends.

"I can only imagine what you're going through." The mother said to Hyon. "If my little Caitlyn ever went missing I'd be in pieces."

"I'm almost in pieces." Hyon replied. "I guess the hope that I have that the police can find her is the glue holding me together."

"You're very strong for still coming out here today."

"Mi Cha and I thought it would be best that we still come and make some art pieces to give to Nari when she returns." Hyon smiled and nodded her head and wiped a little tear away from her cheek.

"Caity has been wondering why Nari isn't here today…"

"It's okay to tell her."

"I don't want to frighten her."

Hyon nodded her head. "Let's just hope that Nari isn't missing for long. Caity won't have to worry for long, Nari will be back soon."

Mi Cha rubbed her glue stick over the spot on the foam rabbit where the nose would go. She made a little round ball with the glue so that glitter would stick to it and create the nose.

"Has anybody seen the black glitter for the nose?" Mi Cha called out to the table.

"No, I can't find the black anywhere." One lady responded.

"Yeah, I saw a spilled pile of some on the table earlier but it's gone now…"

As the final few pieces of candy were placed into the boy's pocket, he came to an opened door at the end of the hall. It was completely dark inside. As the boy entered the room, he flicked on the light switch to see a desk placed directly in front of the doorway. Two feet with pink paws were dangling over the edge. The boy followed the feet up to the black, fur covered legs, pink stomach with the letter **E** sewn on, whiskers, and black bunny ears. The boy ran up to the desk and grabbed hold of the stuffed rabbit. He hugged it close to his face then loosened his grip to look at its cute face.

The boy heard the door suddenly close shut behind him. When he turned around, a life sized version of the black stuffed rabbit stood with its right paw on the door handle. Its left paw rose to its snout as it placed one finger over its lips in a "shhh" gesture.

Outside, a young girl jogged around the playground kicking a soccer ball in front of her. She weaved it in and out between her feet and into the air. Then she threw it onto the roof of the school and watched it roll back down into her arms. She threw it up there again and caught it…threw it again and caught it...threw it up onto the roof a fourth time and waited for it to roll back down. She waited with her arms braced outward to catch it, but it wouldn't come back. The girl held her hand above her eyes to block the sun as she tried to see over the rooftop. She finally decided to walk around to the other side of the building where it most likely landed.

"Yeah nope, haven't seen the black but you could use this last little bit of orange if you'd like." A lady who was sitting beside Mi Cha handed her the almost-empty container of orange glitter. "It'll be an orange nose, but hey, the more colorful the more beautiful, right?"

"Thank you, this should do just fine."

The girl rounded the brick wall corner to the opposite side of the school building. Her soccer ball sat in the lap of an orange stuffed rabbit inside a glowing orange sunspot on the asphalt parking plot.

"Thank you Mr. Rabbit for finding my ball." The girl bent down to grab the soccer ball when she noticed a dark shadow come over the orange sunspot. As she stood up and turned around she was face to face with a large snout and long, droopy ears. The orange colored rabbit cocked its head to the side as it placed one finger over its mouth…

"All right everybody, who is ready for dessert?!" A group of teachers approached the snack table with plates and platters of various kinds of desserts. "All righty, let's see; we've got white chocolate macadamia nut cookies, yellow lemon cheesecake, orange creamsicle popsicles, red velvet cake, dark chocolate fudge, and a gorgeous green key lime pie." One teacher described. "However, I don't think the key lime pie and the red velvet cake will survive for too much longer…because I'll eat it all! Haha. Alright, everybody dig in. We don't want any leftovers!"

As the teachers called the students in for dessert, the ones who were inside the large tube maze struggled to find a way out. A young boy heard the call for dessert and turned to make his way through a small green tube. The sunlight from outside made the green plastic glow as if it were lit up in an emerald glaze. The boy's knees pounded the bottom of the tube as he crawled his way through. Towards the end of the tube, there was a small stuffed rabbit with green fur and the letter **R** on its stomach. The boy grabbed hold of it and peaked through one of the small oval shaped cutaways in the tube for a view outside. The boy peered through and noticed everybody about fifty feet away, huddling around the dessert table with their backs turned towards the playground set. The boy reached his free hand through the opening and waved it around.

"Hey, wait for me! I want some too!"

The boy continued to wave his hand until something clasped hold of it. It was something soft and warm. Through one of the other holes, the boy looked into the large, oval shaped plastic eyes that were staring back at him. A green furry finger rose to the snout, perpendicularly bisecting its lips….

"Anybody want the last piece of red velvet?" A teacher called out to everyone.

"I'll take it!" Hyon raised her hand and took the plate from the teacher. "Red velvet is my favorite. I can make this disappear in the blink of an eye."

At the very top of the playground of plastic tunnels came a tall, curvy red slide. The slide was completely enclosed—a thin tube slide. The outside sunlight pressed against the plastic, making it glow beat red on the inside.

A young girl crawled out from the final tunnel and walked over to the top of the slide to sit down. She ducked her head down inside the tube and gave herself a quick push. She began to slide and curve around the tight edges as the slide descended down to the grass below. All the girl could see was the bright red color of the plastic while she slid down and down.

The girl finally planted her two feet onto the ground as she came to the end of the slide. Ahead of her sat a large stuffed bunny in the grass. It had red fur with the letter **T** sewn onto its stomach. The girl approached it with caution, tilting her head with curiosity. She walked to it, reaching out her arms to grab it. Before she could touch it, a large red paw grabbed hold of the girl's arm from behind. She looked upward to see a red colored rabbit head swaying in the sky. The rabbit moved its hand up to its snout and placed one finger over its lips.

"Alright everybody, dessert is all gone. We finished it all. For the remainder of our time we are going to have our Easter Egg Hunt! There are eggs and candy and much more hidden around the school. If you find it, it's yours! Good luck!"

The group of people disbanded from the dessert table and scampered back to the swings and slides. Others made their way back to the craft table. Hyon stood with Mi Cha against the shaded brick wall of the school as Mi Cha sipped at a cup of iced tea. The teachers worked around the dessert table, cleaning up paper plates and dirty napkins. They had large, white garage bags taped to the sides of the table. Mi Cha watched as a little girl with a wide smile spread over her face approached one of the teachers. The girl and the teacher exchanged a few words before the girl revealed what she was hiding behind her back—a green stuffed bunny. Mi Cha slowly pulled her cup away from her lips and swallowed what she had in her mouth.

"Mom…look." Mi Cha pointed to the little girl with the rabbit.

"Oh yes, that is Caitlyn. She's a good friend of Nari's remember?"

"No not her...look at what she is holding."

"...Oh, it's cute. What about it?"

"It looks very similar to the one that I found in Nari's bed the day she went missing..." Mi Cha dropped her cup into one of the white garage bags and approached Caitlyn.

"Hey Caity, it's Mi Cha."

"Mi mi!" Caitlyn dropped the stuffed rabbit and wrapped her arms around Mi Cha. Her head only went up to the top of Mi Cha's stomach.

"Can you tell me where you found that bunny?"

"...You mean Greenie?" Caitlyn picked up the rabbit and held it out for Mi Cha to see. "It was just sitting inside one of the tubes all by itself. I'm going to give it a home now though."

"...Do you know who it belongs to?"

"No, but it doesn't matter. The rule is finder's keepers, loser's weepers. I found it, so I get to keep it. You can keep an eye on him while I go play though if you want." Caitlyn handed Greenie over to Mi Cha and ran back to the swing sets.

"Is it the same one honey?" Hyon asked.

"Yes, but mine was yellow furred with an **A** on its stomach. This one is green with an **R**."

"...Oh my, I'll call Agent Fischer and let him know." Hyon pulled out her cell phone and dialed Dennis' number.

"Hello, this is Agent Fischer."

"Hey, it's Hyon Park. I'm here at Nari's elementary school for an Easter Decorating party and this girl walked up holding a stuffed rabbit that is very similar looking to the one that was in Nari's bedroom that day…it wasn't her own either. She said she found it in the playground just sitting there."

"…It only makes sense." Dennis responded. "…The kidnapper went after you first, then he went after another family. Each time he kidnapped the youngest child, around the age 5 years old. An elementary school is filled with kids that age. If that *is* the same stuffed bunny, then the kidnapper could very well be at the school right now. Make sure you keep an eye out for any suspicious activity. I'm on my way now, I'll bring the police!"

CHAPTER 3

March 19th 2018

2:00 PM

The sirens grew louder as the blue and red police lights grew brighter. A large black SUV pulled up to the back driveway of the school followed by two police cars. Dennis and Amber exited the vehicle and ran around to the back playground followed by four police officers, including Officer Braidy, Officer Philips, and Officer Browden.

"Who's in charge here?" Dennis called out as he approached the large picnic table.

"I'm the Principal." A man dressed in a blue button down shirt stood up.

"Hi, I'm Agent Fischer of the FBI. You need to put the school under lockdown immediately. We have reason to believe that there is a dangerous kidnapper on these grounds. Tell all the children to go to their parents immediately and for everybody to stay put here in this courtyard until we search the place."

"Oh my god, yes, uh, right away sir!" The principal ran into the school building to initiate lockdown.

"Okay, Officer Braidy, you guard the back of the school, Officer Philips you take the east side, Officer Kelly

you check the inside, and…oh, I don't believe we've met before, what is your name?" Dennis asked when he saw Officer Browden in the group.

"Officer Browden. Tyreese Browden." His dark, bald head gleamed in the bright sunlight.

"Officer Browden, you take the front. Amber and I will stay here on the westward side and keep watch on everybody. Do not let anyone on or off school grounds. Go!"

The officers took their guarding positions that Dennis had ordered them as an announcement came over the loudspeaker:

"Everyone please remain calm, but the school is now under lockdown. Every child please report back to your parent immediately and stay put in the westward courtyard. Anybody inside the building please evacuate to the westward courtyard and remain there until lockdown is over. This is an emergency, please follow all instructions."

A moment of silence heated up before a brew of commotion and chaos came pouring out from the crowd. Children ran from the playground as parents searched for their kid. Children and teachers flooded out of the school building into the courtyard, pushing past the frantic parents. Dennis and Amber pushed through the group of people to the edge of the courtyard where Mi Cha stood wrapped in Hyon's arms. As they approached, Mi Cha pulled away from her mom to hand the green stuffed bunny over to them.

"Yes that's exactly the same as the two others." Amber said pointing to the eyes, ears, and stomach. "How are you two doing?"

"…We're okay. We'll be a lot better if we can finally catch this disgusting animal." Hyon responded.

"If he is *here*, we will catch him. Don't worry."

"Please help!" A lady screamed frantically as she ran up to Dennis. "Please, I, I can't find my daughter anywhere! She was playing soccer over by the tennis courts not very long ago!"

"What does she look like ma'am?"

"Spanish, with long black hair. She was wearing an orange shirt."

"Hey Philips." Dennis radioed in to Officer Philips over his walkie-talkie. "Keep an eye out for a young Spanish girl with long black hair and orange shirt. She was playing soccer over there by the eastern tennis courts."

"…Well I see a soccer ball." Officer Philips replied. "…There's another one of those stuffed rabbits sitting next to it."

"…Yeah, I've got a rabbit over here in the back too by the tube slide." Officer Braidy called in.

"I've got one inside the school. Inside a classroom at the end of the hall." Officer Kelly also called in.

"Okay, so that's a total of what? We have the one from the Parks, one from the European family, the one Mi Cha called us here about, and then we just found 3 more. So that makes six of them so far. Do you see one of them towards the front of the school Officer Browden?" Dennis asked into the walkie-talkie.

"Nope, it's all clear over here Lieutenant."

"So what does this all mean Fischer?" Officer Braidy questioned.

"Unfortunately…unfortunately since the stuffed rabbits are already here it means that the kidnapper just took four more children…he always leaves the stuffed rabbit after he kidnaps them. That means he probably already left here before we could catch him."

"…So we're calling off the lockdown?"

Dennis stood for a moment with the walkie-talkie up to his mouth and looked out at the crowd of parents and children ahead of him. "…Yeah. Call it off. Drop the rabbits off in my car please."

Dennis approached the large group of people crowded around the courtyard. He climbed up onto the top of the nearest picnic table and stood tall so that all eyes were focused on him.

"Listen up people. We believe that four children have just been abducted by a man we call the "Easter Napper". We believe that he already left school grounds so it's safe for you all to leave now. But listen, keep your children close to you at all times. Do not leave them home alone if they are under the age of 10. Based on the pattern so far, we believe that the Easter napper only targets boys and girls around the ages of 4-6, but still, try to take precaution no matter what. I am calling off the lockdown now so I want you all to go home. If you believe that your child is one of the four missing, please speak to one of these officers to set up a missing person file. Thank you."

The crowd dispersed into a flurry of collisions and chaos. People pushed their way up to the front of the

school to get to their cars. Children began crying from all of the noise and confusion. The courtyard finally cleared of people leaving Dennis, Amber, Mi Cha, Hyon, Officer Braidy, Officer Philips, and Officer Kelly behind. They each met in a circle on the black pavement in front of the school's back doors.

"Oh, this is just terrible! Terrible!" Hyon spoke to Amber while her arm was wrapped around Mi Cha. "You've got to do something, what if this just keeps on happening?"

"Mrs. Park, I can assure you we are doing everything that we can. It's not easy. But everything will be okay. Why don't you two go home and relax, okay? There is no way he would go back to your house again, so you are safe, alright?"

Hyon nodded her head and wiped a tear away that was trickling down from her eye. "Okay, okay."

"Alright, do we have everyone here? Where is Officer Browden?" Dennis questioned.

"Browden what's happening over there, everything alright?" Officer Braidy spoke boldly over her walkie-talkie. "Browden! Shit, he's not answering."

"He had the front right? Let's go take a look, maybe something happened to him!" Amber led the group around the side of the school to the front entrance.

A glass window was shattered right beside the front door with a large rock sitting just below it.

"Oh no! Somebody must have broken in!" Amber approached the glass window and inspected it. "What do you think happened to Browden?"

"…It has to be the napper. The napper must have gotten past Browden to get inside the school." Braidy answered.

"My god, how could one person do all this?!" Officer Philips spoke up.

"…Unless it's not just one person." Amber took a step back from the door. "We could very well be dealing with a group of people—at least two or three. Considering how smoothly and intelligently they were able to pull this all off. This isn't your average kidnapper. This is a very well thought out plan. I mean, how could somebody like that go completely unnoticed and kidnap children at a school Easter event with so many other people around?"

"…How about an Easter bunny costume? It would seem like it is just part of the show." Braidy responded.

"Okay, our priorities right now are to get the school dusted for prints and to find Officer Browden—

"Wait!" Amber cut Dennis off. "This window wasn't broken when we first pulled up here. That means someone broke it while the lockdown was in place."

"But if the rabbits were already waiting for us at the time of the lockdown, then why would someone want to break in? They already took the children." Dennis questioned.

"Not break *in*, but maybe they would want to break *out* during the lockdown." Amber explained.

"There aren't any rocks on the inside of the school so that means whoever smashed the window was outside."

"Exactly, so what if someone on the outside helped whoever was on the inside escape out?"

"Who would do that?"

"…Browden does seem to missing a lot of the time right?" Amber asked curiously. "I think it is safe to say that he could be responsible for not only helping the napper escape from the school lockdown here, but also from the jail cell."

"Zando! Amber you are a genius! Officer Braidy, look up the charges that were brought against Zando back when he was first arrested." Dennis ordered.

"On it." Officer Braidy walked back to her police car and pulled up Zando's files on the laptop. "…He was charged for attempted kidnapping and attempted murder on federal agents. You Dennis, you were shot by one of his arrows a few years ago."

"That's it! I remember him now. It was a case I went on with Commander Layton; there were two guys, Zando and Visaki. Layton went after Visaki, while my old Lieutenant and I went after Zando. Visaki was killed but we arrested Zando, so now that he broke out, he must be back to his old business. This is excellent; we now have something to work with! Amber, call Commander Layton and have him put out a search for Officer Browden. Braidy, I want background files on Browden as well—he very well could be assisting Zando in his efforts. All right everybody, we finally have a great lead and sufficient evidence. Let's get to work to fix the kinks and fuse the information together and catch the Easter Napper!"

"They have to mean something..." Dennis sat on his living room couch staring at the six different stuffed rabbits on the floor below. Amber sat in a chair next to him with her legs curled underneath her. She had a laptop sitting on the arm of the chair as she typed.

"It could just be a marker—some sort of sign. Something to let us know that the napper is the one responsible. Maybe they are meant just to mock us; to show us that he can even leave a trail for us but we still can't catch him." Amber responded.

"...Did Braidy ever get all of those missing person files for the children done?"

"I believe so."

"Let me see them."

Amber pulled up the files on her laptop then handed it over to Dennis. He scrolled through each of the files, glancing over the data quickly.

"There's only five files here. We have six rabbits, there should be six missing chidren." Dennis said after looking at the files.

"...Maybe one of them wasn't reported. The first two are the ones we had gotten calls about—Nari and the

European boy Harrison. The other three were reported to Braidy at the elementary school."

"So one of the parents didn't report their child missing."

"IF they are missing. I mean it isn't certain that the stuffed rabbit means that a child was kidnapped, that's just a pattern we found so far."

"No no, there's definitely another child. Maybe the parents just weren't at the school and didn't have a chance to report it yet. Let's wait a few days and see. But let me look at these five that are here."

Dennis browsed through the five files and clicked on their photos and read the information that was presented thus far.

"What are you looking for?" Amber asked him as she peered her head over to look at the screen.

"A connection." Dennis replied.

He paused at one file, then stared at the rabbits, then back at another file, then to the rabbits. His eyes widened with a sudden realization.

"I've got it!"

"What should I do sir? They're catching onto us."

"Do whatever you have to. We only have to make it until Sunday. Easter Sunday. Just as Jesus was reborn, we will have our own king be reborn! It's only a matter of time."

"What is our plan sir?"

"We will strike at the Easter Festival that they are having over on Blakely Island not far from the shore of the state. They will never suspect a thing…"

Dennis walked through the large, plexiglass doors to the main lobby of the FBI headquarters. He wore dark sunglasses over his eyes, but pulled them off as he walked inside. He carried a large, black sack over his right shoulder as he walked to the elevator. The doors slid open as he stuffed the bag through the small opening. A lady dressed in a red buttoned shirt, black skirt, and eyeglasses squeezed inside also.

"What's in the huge bag?" The lady asked.

"…Evidence."

"Oh, I see." The lady nodded her head. "I'm almost done finishing up the Bermuda journal and getting it ready to publish. Probably in another week or so it should be all set. I just have to get a few more sections edited and approved by the publication company. Would you like to check it out so far?"

"I can't. I'm working on an investigation. Just send a proof copy to my house. I'll take a look at it when I can."

"Sure thing Lieutenant."

The elevator came to a stop at the 2nd floor. Dennis made his way to a large area that was filled with desks and cubicles. Computers beeped and buzzed, phones rang, and high heels clapped against the marble floors as people scampered around. Computer screens displayed mazes of coordinate locations and satellite images. Others displayed profiles of suspected persons. The Agents worked around the room as if they were honey bees in command by the Queen, who lived in the office on the elevated platform in the middle of the room. The platform was circular in shape and was surrounded by blurred glass. There were three stairs on the platform leading to a door in the glass. Inside was Commander Layton. Dennis walked inside and shut the door behind him—closing out the beeps and ringing noises of the hive.

Commander Layton sat in his leather chair with a cup of coffee in his hand. He sat up as Dennis pulled out a chair and threw the black bag onto it. One by one Dennis reached inside and pulled out each of the stuffed rabbits. He sat them in a single file line on the commander's desk; each one facing towards Layton. First the yellow one with the letter A, then the white one with the letter E, then the

orange one with the letter S, then the black one with another letter E, then the green one with the letter R, and lastly the red one with the letter T. All six colored rabbits sat on the desk facing towards Commander Layton.

"...What the hell is this all about Fischer?"

"The kidnapper left these. One for each child that he kidnapped. Do you notice anything special about them?"

"...Uh, no. No I don't. Care to explain?"

"Watch this." Dennis picked up the rabbits and arranged them into a new order. First the white one with the letter E, then the yellow one with the A, then the orange one with the S, then the red one with the T, then the black one with the E, and lastly the green one with the R. "Notice anything now?"

"...They spell out Easter." The Commander leaned back in his big leather chair and twiddled a pen in his hands.

"Exactly." Dennis said enthusiastically.

"Would you mind telling me how this helps out the investigation in any way?"

"Well for one, whenever there is a specific pattern like this it usually means that they have a set route. The napper must know *who* he wants and for *what* reason. These are not just some random kidnappings—there is a deeper purpose. Now, I also took a look at each of the missing children's files and they each happen to come from a particular ethnic family—distinctly ethnic. If you take a look at the rabbits' colors, I believe that they symbolize

each child's ethnicity." Dennis reached into his black bag and pulled out six photographs of the missing children.

"Harrison Hensley—a European white boy. In his home remained the *white* fur rabbit." Dennis leaned the photograph up against the bunny's stomach.

"Nari Park—an Asian girl from South Korea. In her home remained the yellow rabbit."

Commander Layton watched with curiosity.

"Sophia Gomez—a Spanish girl. She received the orange rabbit. Reuben Moore—a Ticonderoga Native American, received the red rabbit. Now for the black rabbit, I don't have a match just yet, but that's because only five children were reported to be missing; I believe that a sixth one was kidnapped though. But lastly, Tony Morelli—an Italian from Rome, received the green rabbit. The letters on the stomachs also correspond with the first letter of the ethnicity. E for European, A for Asian, S for Spanish, T for Ticonderoga, the E is missing for now, and R for Roman."

"…Well. This case just got a whole lot deeper. Do you know the purpose for all this?" The Commander questioned.

"I don't know why or for what purpose, but I'm positive that the kidnapper needs these *specific* children for some reason. However, since all six letters of the word Easter are already spelled out with the rabbit, I think that he already kidnapped everybody that he needs; I'm certain that he won't strike again. What we need to do now is catch him before he harms any of those kids. Amber and I, along with Officer Braidy, came to the conclusion that

Zando is our greatest suspect for the kidnapper. And we have firm belief that Officer Browden is the culprit who is assisting Zando in his efforts."

"Hm, so what do you think we should do now?"

"Right now let's put our focus on finding Browden."

"We can't put our focus on Browden over Zando." The Commander replied. "That will be a waste of time and by then those kids could be dead!" He stood up front his seat.

"Zando will be too difficult to find; he is skilled. He knows exactly what he is doing. And we have just about zero information on him except for his previous attempt as kidnapping a few years ago. Browden we can find. We have his files, we know where he lives, what he is like…we can find him easily. If we do find him, he should be able to better lead us to Zando, who will then lead us to the kids." Dennis explained.

Commander Layton paced in a circle next to his chair for a few moments while clicking the cap of his pen up and down. "Alright then…let's focus on finding Officer Browden."

"As Easter Sunday approaches, we see the children getting antsy and the parents bustling around to prepare for the holiday. The annual Easter Festival will

take place yet again on Blakely Island. Ferry tickets are selling out fast, so if you want to take part in this year's grand festival, hurry up and buy your tickets *today*. Like always, the Island will be completely decorated in correspondence to Easter—there will be lights, music, egg hunts, candy, desserts, and even the Easter Bunny himself, Peter Cottontail, will make an appearance! We hope you can take part in this wonderful gathering. And don't forget the true meaning of the celebration—the rebirth of our leader. He gives us life. Without him, the community would fall apart. May he be with you all. Thank You."

This broadcast was brought to you by the Seattle City Council in correspondence with…Glad—the best scented wax candles around.

The black SUV pulled up the cement driveway as Dennis turned the radio off. A police car followed close behind, pulling up alongside the SUV. Dennis, Amber, Officer Braidy and Officer Philips emerged from the vehicles and made their way up to the front porch door of the house. They marched past the black lettering on the front wall that read *Browden*. Dennis led the way to the front door with his gun drawn. Amber followed and pulled out a small hair pin as she reached the door knob.

"Just like good old times." Amber smiled and waved the pin in front of Dennis' eyes. She then stuck it into the key hole and twirled it around until the lock clicked open. Dennis jerked the door open with a push from his right shoulder and the group charged inside.

It was dark; the lights were off and all the blinds and curtains were drawn. Amber flicked on a few lamps as the others rounded the house. The furniture was old and rustic looking. A small box TV set sat on the floor facing the torn up wicker sofa. The coffee table was made of unfinished splintery wood and the carpets were all stained and torn. Through the archway to the next room, was the kitchen. Amber walked in and examined the old looking appliances and cheap wooden table. There was no washing machine or electric stove; just a small fire oven, refrigerator, and a few small appliances on the counter.

"Hey Amber, come check this out!" Dennis called from what sounded like a room in the back of the house. Amber made her way down the narrow hallway to reach Dennis' faint voice. She came to a small bedroom with nothing in it but a mattress on the floor, a small wooden dresser, and a closet. Dennis stood hovering in front of the opened closet door, looking down.

"What is it?" Amber questioned as she made her way over to him. Dennis signaled a hand down to the floor of the closet where a black fur colored bunny costume lay—the body part was clumped up while the head sat, glaring up at the two of them with its piercing red eyes.

"Here's our proof…Browden is definitely working together with Zando. Philips, come and get this thing put away for evidence!"

Officer Philips came running into the room with a large plastic bag and latex gloves on. He gathered the costume into a ball and stuffed it inside the bag and sealed it tight.

"Did you find anything else?" Dennis asked Officer Braidy when they met in the hallway.

"I did. I found this little note on the sink counter in the bathroom. The handwriting is messy, but I believe it says *Easter Island Sunday night at 9 PM.*"

"Sunday night…that's the night of the Easter Festival."

"Exactly. And who is going to be at the Easter Festival?" Officer Braidy asked, although she already knew the answer.

Dennis nodded his head. "Kids."

"You think they will plan to strike again at the Festival?" Amber questioned.

"It would be the perfect time to." Braidy answered. "Lots of commotion, noise, nobody would expect it. It would be pretty easy for them to take some more kids without being caught."

Dennis nodded in agreement. "Okay. We'll have to gather a team to go there this Sunday and form a parameter around the festival area. Until it ends, we'll make sure that nobody gets in, and nobody gets out…"

"How are you holding up, baby?"

"I'm okay…but still scared." Mi Cha sat comfortably on Anthony's lap on the couch. The TV was

on, but the volume was too soft to hear. All of the lights were off, except for the light of a small lamp on the table at the side of the couch. Mi Cha pulled her knees up close to her body and rested her head on Anthony's left shoulder.

"Are you tired?"

Mi Cha lifted her head up and blinked a few times. "No, not really. I haven't been able to sleep too well."

"Do you want to do something to lift the mood?"

"Um, like what?"

"I don't know, just something." Anthony slid his hand down Mi Cha's back and over the tight black shorts she had on.

Mi Cha bit her lip slightly as his hand stopped and squeezed her butt. "…I don't know, what if it hurts?"

"It shouldn't hurt too badly. Plus you'll have to do it eventually."

Mi Cha smiled, "That's true. And maybe it will help relieve my tension."

"Of course. And you'll be tired after we do it so you could finally get some sleep."

"Well, sounds good to me then, haha."

Anthony smirked and pinched the bottom corners of Mi Cha's pink shirt between his fingers. He pulled it up, over her body and over her head until her white lace bra appeared underneath. Mi Cha then took hold of the shirt and pulled it down her arms and threw it onto the floor below. Anthony wrapped his arms around Mi Cha's

stomach, pulling her in close to his body. He reached his hands up, behind her back until he felt the soft lace of her bra. He worked his fingers to the middle and unhooked it. The straps slid down halfway off her slender shoulders until Mi Cha pulled them all the way down. She threw the bra on top of the shirt that was lying on the floor.

Anthony reached his hands to Mi Cha's front side and ran them across her body. He felt the soft, smoothness of her chest as his hands cupped her breasts.

"How do they feel?" Mi Cha asked softly.

"Great."

"Good…now let me feel you." Mi Cha smiled slightly and sat up a bit. Anthony stared into her hazel, almond shaped eyes as she slid her hand down underneath his shorts.

Dylan A.

CHAPTER 4

March 20th 2018

1:00 PM

The large, yellow lift screeched as it raised the man into the air. He wore a yellow hard-hat and a shiny reflective vest. Wrapped neatly around his hand and elbow, was a strand of fluorescent, pastel colored lights. The lift stopped moving when the man reached the top of a wooden pole. He placed the end of the strand onto the flat surface of the wood and tried to staple it down with a staple gun in his opposite hand. When he let go of the end of the strand, it began to fall to the ground below and he saw that the staple didn't punch through the wood all the way. The lights fell down like a green vine through the trees and landed on the grass where it almost blended right in.

"Dammit!" The man said as he reached down onto the floor of the lift to grab another wound up strand. He placed the end onto the wooden pole again and stapled it down several times and didn't let go until he was sure it was snug.

Below the man, several people scurried about the large, open field. Surrounding the area of naked grass were thick green trees and plants. They created a dense forest around the bare clearing. Cardboard boxes lay scattered on the grass, as the decorators hurried to and from them.

Plastic eggs, lights, stuffed animals, paints, pink and yellow colored grass, streamers, and baskets all exploded out from the boxes and took their places throughout the grassy field. Tables and chairs, stands, and games were also being set up by the decorators.

At the front of the island, several large tropical trees sat facing out towards the sea. Waves brushed up against the rough, rocky wall of the island. A fair sized boat floated in the water near a long wooden dock which led up to the clearing.

Past the forest of trees and over some hills just a few miles up from the clearing, came a large hidden grotto. The grotto was enclosed by a small wall made of leaves and twigs and large branches. Inside, seven men stood. Six of them were standing in a group, while one of them was standing in front of them all. The man in the front wore a plain white t-shirt and black pants. He had a light beard, with dark hair, and hazel green eyes.

"Listen up." He called.

The other six people silenced themselves and listened intently.

"In just a few days, the time will come. I know that you are feeling anxious and excited…maybe even a little nervous, but the wait won't be for much longer. That's right, this Easter Sunday our lord will rise again and we will forever triumph…however, while this is one of our great goals, let us not forget the other part of our mission—revenge." There was a pause in his speech as he walked to the left a bit. "Browden. I am aware that your police station is onto us…is this true?"

"Yes. And they have the FBI involved too. That damn son of a bitch Dennis Fischer."

"Fischer…the same one who was teamed up with Commander Layton years ago?"

"The same one. The one that tried to kill Zando!"

"…I see. Well…I'm putting you in charge of getting revenge. The rest of us will see that our lord rises peacefully."

"…How can I do that alone? Can't anyone else help?"

"It takes six of us on Easter Sunday. That means one other must be the one who takes revenge on our lord's killer. You know what you have to do, we already hid the Easter eggs." The man in white spoke more boldly.

"I understand. I'll do it in the name of our lord Visaki!"

3:00 PM

The court room filled with people. The judge was led up to his desk in the front. His black robe engulfed his chair like a large sheet. He rested his hands on the desktop in a folded position as Dennis and Amber filed into the first row of seats on the left side of the aisle. A group of legal officials sat together on the right side.

The judge straightened some papers on his desk and held them up at an angle away from his eyes so he could read from them.

"Lieutenant Fischer and Agent Berns, please rise and give your opening statement please." His voice was low and raspy.

Dennis and Amber stood and made their way into the center of the room in front of the judge. Commander Layton sat loosely in the row behind them, accompanied by others from the FBI headquarters. Layton's sleeves were rolled up to his elbows and his arm rested on the back of the bench. His right leg was propped up on his left knee.

"Your honor, Amber and I, and the rest of the Seattle FBI station have decided to publish a journal, *Bermuda*, which details everything that happened during those few months on the island. I know this sounds like a cheap shot, but with our current on-going investigation of the Easter kidnappers we would like to delay this hearing until we can get the journal finished and published. We will present to the court information from that journal that is necessary while anyone who wants to can read it to learn the full amount of information for themselves."

"...You do realize that the entire city is suspicious about your station don't you? It's been over a year now and still no word about what exactly happened on Bermuda. All we know is that the entire island has disappeared into the water. The people are sick of waiting in wonder. We want answers Fischer."

"Yes we know." Amber responded. Her blonde hair was tied back in a bun and she wore a maroon colored suit with white blouse underneath. "The journal will be out very soon. I promise. But until then, all I will say is that what happened on Bermuda was unlike anything we ever saw before. It's going to sound pretty crazy, and some people may not believe it, but we can assure you that everything written in the journal actually happened. It was written based on Dennis' experiences since he kept log of everything that took place each day while he was there. It's a primary source with all his information and thoughts during his mission there. It's 100% accurate as the events happened."

"I see...well...how soon are we talking here for this journal to be finished? Or are you just trying to stall us out in order to come up with some answers?" The judge asked suspiciously.

"No. We are not stalling." Dennis spoke up and turned towards everyone in the court room. "The journal will be ready shortly and then you will all know the real story of the Bermuda Triangle."

11:30 PM

The house was quiet and dark; Dennis and Amber were inside their bedroom sleeping soundly. A soft light above the kitchen counter was left on, casting a faint hue of yellow throughout the house. The curtains were drawn over the large windows above the sink, however, a black shadow appeared behind them. It was the shadow of a large man who appeared to be coming closer to the window. His shadow raised its arm, revealing something large and round within his hand. The shadow smacked the glass of the window and it shattered on impact; large shards of glass fell down onto the kitchen counter and inside the sink.

The curtains were pushed to the side as a dark hand reached its way inside, grabbing hold of the edge of the window sill. A body then appeared dressed in black clothing with the butt of a gun sticking out from his belt. The man hoisted himself through the window and threw his legs over, across the countertop. His feet landed onto the tiled floor below without making a sound. His dark face gleamed with a look of rage and determination; Browden has come for his revenge.

He made his way silently through the kitchen until he came to the large staircase leading to the next floor. Each step he took with extreme caution, trying not to make any creaking or footstep sounds. He drew his gun as the final few steps neared and quickened his pace into the hallway. There were several doors—two of them were closed, one was opened. The opened door Browden saw, despite the darkness, that it was a bathroom. He slowly turned the knob of the first closed door that was on the opposite side of the bathroom and pointed the barrel of his gun inside—just a small closet—then pulled back out and closed it. The final door was at the end of the hallway and this, he was sure, was Dennis' bedroom.

He turned the knob slowly and pushed the door open without a sound. Inside the room he stepped with the barrel of his gun aimed right towards the center of the bed. Through the darkness, he could make out two small lumps under the covers and pointed the gun towards the one on the left side first. He pulled the trigger—once, twice—then aimed at the other lump—one, two shots again—then he lowered his weapon.

A shadow sprang from the corner of the room behind the door and plowed into Browden from the left side. He tumbled over, his gun slid across the floor. The shadow pinned him to the ground as another shadow swooped out from the right corner and retrieved the fallen weapon. The sound of the loaded weapon pointed towards him caused Browden to stop struggling and lay still.

"Don't move!" The shadow holding the gun yelled, as it glided across the room towards the light switch near the door.

The lights flicked on and revealed the faces of three people in the room. Amber at the light switch with the gun aimed at Browden, who was pinned to the floor by Dennis.

"Browden!" Dennis yelled.

"I shot you!" Browden replied. "I shot both of you. In the bed!"

"We heard the sound of the window shattering downstairs and figured that we would hide and wait to ambush whoever tried to come attack us." Amber moved closer and lowered the weapon.

"Now we got you Browden! We know you are working together with Zando. We know that you are the one who let him out of his jail cell since it was *you* who was supposed to be keeping watch of that section of cells. Now that we caught you, we're bringing you to the station. You're going to tell us where we can find Zando!"

Police officers arrived to the house and hand cuffed Zando. They walked him outside to the cop car to bring him over to the FBI station. Dennis and Amber threw on some clothes and clipped their badges to their jackets then followed the police to the headquarters with their own vehicle. As they pulled up to the building, the officers were already inside and had Browden seated at a table in the interrogation room. Dennis and Amber entered the room together.

"You see, the problem officials like us have," Dennis said as he paced back and forth in front of the table that Browden was seated at, "is that, although we are smarter than you guys and are able to figure out your plans—every secret you're trying to keep, we can find—it's still always so difficult for us to pinpoint a *motive*. We know you're working with Zando for instance. We know that it was you guys who kidnapped the six children and left the stuffed rabbits behind. We *know* that. What we don't know is, *why?* Why children? Why six of them? Why, Mr. Browden, are they all from different ethnic backgrounds and why did the stuffed rabbit they received coordinate to that?"

Amber leaned against the wall and watched Browden's facial reactions as Dennis questioned him.

"…We need them." Browden replied solemnly.

"Need them…and need them for WHAT, I'm asking."

"It's none of your concern Mr. Fischer."

"Innocent children kidnapped is *completely* of my concern! My job is to protect—protect the innocent people of the city from monsters like you and Zando!"

"Where can we find Zando?" Amber spoke for the first time.

"Haha, you're very funny Ms. Berns." Browden let out a smile and tiled his head back.

"The Easter festival, Sunday night at 9PM, right? We found the note in your house."

"Answer her questions!" Dennis leaned in after Browden wouldn't say anything.

"Hahaha," Browden rested his elbows on the tabletop and leaned his body inward as well, "You guys really don't understand, do you? It doesn't matter if you catch Zando or not…our plans will still be fulfilled."

6:00 AM

Hyon slid the covers off of her body and swung her feet over the side of the bed. She looked at the bright, red glow of the alarm clock on her nightstand—6:00 AM. Ever since Nari had been taken, she had been waking up earlier and earlier; partly because she was nervous and afraid, and partly because she held hope that one day she would wake up to a call from Agent Fischer with news that they had found Nari and captured the monster who took her. She wanted more than anything to see that man locked behind bars for the rest of his life—or maybe even something worse.

This morning, when she checked her phone, she saw that there had been a missed call from around one in the morning. She recognized the number as Dennis' and quickly dialed it back as she slipped her feet into a pair of slippers which were sitting by the foot of the bed.

"Agent Fischer, it's me. I was sleeping so I missed when you called. Is there something you have to tell me?"

"Amber and I had our house broken into last night—

"Are you guys okay? What happened?"

"It was Browden. He tried to assassinate us, but we got him apprehended and brought him over to headquarters last night for interrogation."

"He's the one who took Nari?!" Hyon spoke with a small tremble in her voice; from excitement and nervousness.

"He's the one who helped Zando escape from prison. We can't say which of the two is the one who took your daughter, but they were certainly both working together and have the same goals we believe."

"Did you find any new information or clues, or anything from him that'll help you find Nari?"

"Unfortunately, no. He wouldn't tell us much. It looks like we are going to stick with our original plan of waiting until the Easter Festival to find Zando. With Browden detained here at headquarters, it'll be our entire team against one."

"Should I stay home or go to the festival with you guys that day? I mean…that might be where they brought Nari." Hyon asked.

"If you do come, be sure to blend in with the crowd."

Hyon made her way downstairs. The morning sunrise cast a hue of pink light through the living room windows. Mi Cha was laying on the couch, cuddled next to Anthony, with a thin blanket halfway slid off, onto the floor. Hyon picked it up and covered the two of them before taking the empty snack bowls and cups from the coffee table. She placed them in a pile next to the sink and grabbed some bread to pop into the toaster. She poured some coffee into the pot and pushed the button on to start brewing.

The small commotion from the kitchen was enough to stir Anthony from his sleep—he was a light sleeper. Mi Cha's arms were wrapped lightly around his neck, but not strong enough that he couldn't pull them off. He lightly moved her off of him as he sat up and got off of the couch. He made his way through the living room and into the kitchen where Hyon was standing, staring down at the coffee pot.

"Ms. Park," Anthony started.

"Jesus!" Hyon jumped back and turned around. "You scared me, I thought you were asleep."

"I heard some noise in the kitchen." He moved to the refrigerator and grabbed the container of orange juice. "Plus, I never liked sleeping on couches anyway." He let out a slight smile.

"I just heard some news from the FBI Agent who's working on the case. I was going to tell you and Mi Cha when you woke up."

Anthony poured the orange liquid into a clear glass, all the way up to the brim. "She's still sleeping. What's the news?"

"They've captured Browden."

"Officer Browden? My dad used to talk to me about him."

"That's right, your dad works at the local police station too doesn't he?"

"Officer Philips. He used to tell me how Browden would always miss work and never explain why. He was always super quiet—not in the shy way, but like, the creepy way. He always seemed too much in his own world, my dad would say. He also used to read all these creepy books during lunch breaks and stuff."

Hyon popped the toast out of the toaster and began spreading butter over the crispy surface. "Creepy books?"

"Some African tribal stuff, I don't know. I'm just saying, he was creepy. If any of the officers there would have let Zando out, I'm not surprised it's Browden." Anthony replaced the juice container back inside the fridge and leaned his back against the counter sipping from the glass. "Although, I don't really see how." He said before taking a long gulp.

"How what?"

"How Browden could have let Zando out."

"What do you mean?"

"He was just one of the guards. Only the Chief has access to the keys for the cells. If the guards want access into one, they need to ask permission to use the key. So Browden couldn't have let Zando unless the chief knew about it."

Hyon threw the dirty butter knife into the sink and ran hot water over it. "Well, who's the chief?"

"Officer Braidy." Anthony set his empty orange juice glass next to the dirty bowls and headed back into the living room.

7:30 AM

"What are you planning to do?" Dennis asked Amber as they walked together down the hall of the FBI station. Amber's black suit jacket flew open in the air as she glided around the corners. She carried a sheet of blank printer paper and a pencil in her hand.

"I have an idea." She said as they made their way to the holding room for Browden. Inside, he was sitting motionless in a chair with his hands cuffed in his lap. A table was present in front of him. Amber slapped the paper and pencil down onto the table top.

"Uncuff him." She said to the guard who had let them into the room.

When Browden's hands were free, Amber stepped up beside him as Dennis and the other officer stood watching.

"Tomorrow night is the Easter Festival." Amber began.

"You're letting me free so I can go celebrate my favorite holiday?" Browden cracked a smile.

"That's what Zando is going to think."

Dennis narrowed his eyes, trying to understand what Amber was getting at.

"I brought this paper and pencil here. You're going to write a note to your friend Zando telling him to meet you at a specific location on the island Sunday night."

"So you are letting me free then?" Browden asked again.

"Are you going to write this letter or not?" Amber folded her arms in front of her chest.

Browden licked his lips and rubbed his face with his hands a few moments before answering. "Now, why should I help you?"

"Because you're already captured. You can't go anywhere. You may have been there to let Zando out of jail, but now there's nobody else who's going to let you free. We already know that you two were planning another strike during the Easter festival, so we are going to have a team of officers surrounding the entire perimeter. It's Zando against all of us; there's no way he can do anything. Your plans are coming to an end. So, you can either write this letter to make our jobs just a tiny bit easier, or, you don't write it and we catch Zando anyway. Your choice…'Officer'." Amber straightened the paper and pushed the pencil closer to his hand.

Dennis watched as Browden's eyes shifted back and forth between the paper and the pencil, and as he closed, and opened them again. Amber gave a quick glance at Dennis who nodded back in approval.

Browden cleared his throat and took up the pencil in his hand. "What do you want it to say?"

Amber smiled—first at Browden, then back at Dennis. "Tell him that before you begin whatever plans you have in mind, that there is something very important you have to tell him. And that you want him to meet you by the big tropical trees at the South end of the island."

9:00 PM

“That was a good idea today with the letter. Nice job talking him in to writing it.” Dennis grabbed Amber by the waist as they entered their house and kissed her.

“Yeah, smart thinking, right?”

“Just like old times.” Dennis smiled and kissed her again. They slipped their jackets off and hung them on the coat rack by the door. Amber slipped back into Dennis’ arms.

“Do we have everything ready for tomorrow?” She asked.

“Officer Braidy has her team all set to go. We have our team set to go. You and I will head to the trees at the South end in hopes that Zando will show up there like Browden put in the letter. If not, we know he’ll be somewhere on the island and we can find him then.”

“…You think it’ll be that easy?”

“An entire team of Officers and FBI agents versus one nut job sounds pretty easy of a battle to me.” Dennis smiled.

Amber pulled away from his grasp slightly. “I don’t know, I just feel like something is missing. It shouldn’t have been this easy of a set up.”

“They’re a couple of freaks kidnapping children before Easter, how difficult do you think it would be?”

"I know that you know what I'm talking about. Something in your gut must be talking to you like it is to me."

"Well…what is it telling you?" Dennis held Amber's hands.

"We don't know the motive behind their actions. What if they are something more than just some freaks kidnapping children? Why on Easter? What's the significance?"

"I would love to find out the motive just as much as you, but the priority right now needs to be capturing Zando and finding the missing children. We have a great lead, a great set up with the letter you had Browden write, let's just focus on Zando for now."

"There's still time before the festival. I think I want to go over some things again just to make see if there's anything else I can find…have you spoken with Hyon yet?"

"She called me back earlier today. I told her we had Browden in custody."

"That's good." Amber bent down and pulled her heels off of her feet and placed them down on the floor mat by the door, under the coats. "I'm going to go look through some things in the office."

"You sure you don't want to get some rest?" Dennis said.

"I will. I just want to make sure that nothing is being overlooked. Is Hyon coming to the festival tomorrow?"

"Her and Mi Cha."

"You think the missing children will be there?" Amber asked with a somber tone.

"…I don't know."

Amber nodded slowly and turned back down the hall towards the office.

Dylan A.

CHAPTER 5

Easter Sunday

12:00 PM

Everyone was gathered in the meeting room at the FBI headquarters. Commander Layton stood at the head of the table, with Dennis and Amber on each side of him. Other Agents sat around the table, with Officer Braidy, Officer Philips, and other police officers from the station, standing around it. The six different colored stuffed rabbits sat in a line at the head of the table. An air of determination and confidence swept across the room as they talked over their plan once again. Today was Easter Sunday—the day of the Easter festival on Blakely Island. Dennis and Amber were determined to make a clean capture of Zando before he could kidnap any more children, or do any more harm to the ones already in his possession. There was no way of knowing whether they would be able to free the six children alive, or find them at all, but capturing Zando was the main goal. If they couldn't find the children, then perhaps Zando could help lead them in the right direction. One step must be taken at a time during an investigation. It is unlikely to solve everything in one piece; instead, the puzzle pieces come together one at a time, and Zando was the next piece of the puzzle that had to be filled.

"The six rabbits sitting here represent the six missing children." Commander Layton began speaking to the Agents and Officers. "We don't know whether the children will be there on the island with Zando or not, but it sure as hell is worth it to look. We're going to have the entire place surrounded, that means I want you all to keep a look out, not only for Zando, but for the children also. You each have their names and photographs on file on your phones—take a good look and remember what they look like. Everyone here is going to be using the same radio wave on your walkie-talkies, so if you see something, you report it immediately." Layton bent down slightly and clutched the back of a chair. "We want this to be a clean and easy mission—that means keep your fingers off the damn trigger unless it's absolutely necessary." He stood up straight again and gestured toward Dennis. "That's all from me. Lieutenant Fischer has details of where each of you will be stationed around the island. Go ahead Fischer."

Dennis took the Commander's standing spot at the head of the table. "Agent Herman, you will be at the Northwest corner in the woods just above the festival. Agent Clyde, you will be at the Northeast corner. Agent Simon, you will be at the Southwest corner, and lastly, Agent Palmer, you will be at the Southeast corner. Each of you four Agents will be accompanied by two other officers who will position themselves about thirty meters away on the left and right sides of you. And each of those officers will have others thirty meters away from them. This will create a fan-like circular barrier that should cover the perimeter of where the festival is going to take place." Dennis turned, first to Amber, then to Officer Braidy. "Agent Berns and Officer Braidy will be accompanying me to the location at the South end of the island where we will be expecting Zando to meet us. If for some reason he doesn't show up there, we will radio in and look for him elsewhere. Like the commander said, we want this to be smooth and easy. As long as everyone sticks to the plan and we communicate to each other if there is any issue, everything should work out." Dennis moved his way closer to Amber. "Agent Berns and I were able to solve the mystery of Bermuda with help only from the late Lieutenant Vera, and without any solid planning. With all of us working together to find *one* guy, we should have no problems at all. Now, the ferry to Blakely Island leaves in just over an hour; you should all have time to grab whatever you need to from your homes, but please head over to the dock right after. Okay, that should have covered everything. As long as everyone understands what they have to do, you're free to go." He ended his speech with a smile and a nod and took Amber's hand as they left the headquarters.

"Hi, is this Mr. Phillips? Great, this is Ms. Park, Mi Cha's mother. Anthony told me that you had noticed Browden always reading some weird, African tribal books. I was just wondering if you knew anything more about that. It might help the case."

"Yeah, uh, they were some really strange looking books he read. I don't know the actual name of them or anything specific though, I'm sorry." Officer Philips replied over the phone.

"Could you perhaps look into it? Or report it to your team or to the FBI so they could do some research on it. It might be insignificant but it just struck me as something that could be worth looking into, and anything could be a help, you know?"

"I can report it Officer Braidy right now."

"No," Hyon said, "Not her. I'd rather it be reported to the FBI. Commander Layton, is that his name? Tell him about it. Have his team investigate it further."

"Braidy is the chief of the station, she was much closer to Browden than any of us, and especially more so than the FBI. She might even know the name of the books already without even investigating."

"That's the problem Mr. Philips." Hyon replied.

"Excuse me?"

"There's no solid evidence showing that Browden was the one who let Zando out. So for now, I don't trust any of the officers that work at the station—with the exception of you, because your son is my daughter's boyfriend. Can you promise me you'll alert Layton and his team, nobody else?"

"…Sure thing Ms. Park. Although, if they do find anything from it, Braidy is sure to find out. The officers at the station are working together with the FBI agents. Perhaps I just shouldn't report it."

"I want it reported please. That's fine if Braidy finds out eventually, just make sure that if they do find anything that Agent Fischer finds out first."

Hyon hung up the phone as Mi Cha entered the bedroom. A suitcase was sitting on top of the bed with some clothes packed into it. Mi Cha took a look at them noticed that they were Nari's clothes.

"You're packing Nari's stuff?" Mi Cha asked.

Hyon turned from the bed to face Mi Cha who was standing in the doorway. "…When they find Nari on the island, I want to have fresh clothes ready for her."

"Mom," Mi Cha advanced further and placed her hand on top of Hyon's, "What if they don't find her?"

"Just to be sure." Hyon turned away from Mi Cha and walked over to her closet. "Go finish getting ready, the ferry leaves in less than an hour."

6:30 PM

A stream of men and women in black suits trickled past the security check at the marina and began to board the ferry. The Agents and Officers filled the seats at the front of the boat, while other family passengers filled the rest. The children all boarded with excited faces ready for the Easter bash on the island. Candy, chocolate, baskets, music, dancing, Peter Cottontail—a child's Easter paradise. The Agents and Officers were boarding for a mission; a mission to find Zando and ensure that everyone at the festival stays safe. Then there were Hyon and Mi Cha who were caught in between; they wouldn't be boarding to celebrate and they also wouldn't be on a mission. Instead, they would be in the middle of the two realms, waiting to find their place. Despite everyone's differing objectives, they were all aboard the same ferry, heading to the same location. Next stop: Easter Island.

"All passengers please fasten your seatbelts while the boat first takes off." The voice over the inter-com spoke as the seatbelt light flashed on. The Agents, however, already had their seatbelts on before the warning came across; their careers are all about being one step ahead. Dennis had reached over and grabbed Amber's hand as the boat started to pick up speed.

"You nervous?" He asked her.

"About the boat ride or about the mission?" She smiled.

"Either."

"Last time we were on a boat it crashed through the Bermuda triangle." She squeezed his hand tighter.

The boat picked up speed and rolled over the deep blue waters. Small water droplets from the waves splashed up, over the railing until the water smoothed out. Amber watched the water for a while as the boat sped across it. Then she pulled her laptop out from her bag and opened it on her lap.

"What are you looking for now?" Dennis asked.

"Just going through some stuff again. Nothing in particular."

"You sure? Because the past few days you've been pretty immersed in your research. You must be on to something."

"...Okay. I've been reviewing some of the security footage from the Seattle police station." Amber spoke softly and leaned her head in towards Dennis so that nobody else could hear.

"You mean the original tape of Zando disappearing from his cell?"

"No, not just that one. Look at this." Amber moved the laptop over between her and Dennis, and zoomed in on an image of a security guard walking through the halls. She zoomed the image it in until just the guard's belt and keys filled the entirety of the screen.

"What am I looking at?"

"Keys. They're attached to his belt. But they are all keys for cells."

"What are you getting at?"

"I've looked at a lot of these tapes and all of the security guards have a set of keys like this for the cells. These are the *only* keys they have on them though. If Browden was a security guard like them, then he should have only had keys to the cells."

"Which is how he let Zando out. We knew that already."

"Then how did he get into the security camera room to edit the tapes if he only had keys to the cells? I called the station and asked, and they told me that the only person with access to the camera room is the *chief* officer." Amber whispered quietly to Dennis.

"Officer Braidy?"

Amber nodded.

"Browden could have easily stolen the keys at some point. Let's not make assumptions here." Dennis shook his head.

"I agree." Amber closed her laptop. "Then let's not make the assumption that Officer Browden worked alone to free Zando."

The ferry began to slow down as it approached Blakely Island. The thick green of the grass and forest of the island came into view. The row of large tropical trees could be seen in the distance. The festival was to take place just north of the trees. As the boat came into dock and pulled to a stop, everyone trickled their way down, onto the wooden dock. The Agents and Officers were the first to exit and all congregated in a circle on the dirt shore. Dennis checked his wristwatch and spoke to the group.

"Okay everyone. We have exactly half an hour until the official start of the festival. That means that we have to get prepared and get into our positons quickly. Some of you have a little ways to walk if you are going to be in the northern areas, so make sure you get there quick enough. I want to have a small meeting by the trees over there before we start heading to our spots, but first, does anybody have any last minute questions?"

"I have something to tell you in private, Lieutenant." Officer Philips spoke up from the group.

"Sure thing. Everyone else, you're free to do whatever you want, but meet up by the trees in exactly five minutes."

The group of Agents and Officers cleared out, leaving Dennis and Amber alone with Officer Philips.

"Is it something super private or can Agent Berns hear too?" Dennis asked.

"Ms. Park called me last night and requested that I ask for an investigation into the books that Browden used to read. I told her I'd ask Officer Braidy about it, but she said that she didn't trust Braidy. She said there's no real evidence that Browden let Zando out and that maybe Braidy is the one who did it. She was the chief after all."

"Was the chief?" Dennis asked.

"She is the chief I meant. But I'm just saying, I don't know if we should trust Braidy."

"Amber brought up a concern about her too, but I don't think we have the time right now to really worry about this. Amber and I will be with Braidy so she won't be able to do anything even if she is in on it."

"Just be careful." Officer Philips said as he began to walk away. "Braidy was pretty close with Browden."

"Okay, thanks for letting me know your concern. Now let's get going. It's almost time."

Hyon and Mi Cha exited from the dock and onto the dirt walkway of the island. Hyon was wearing a long maroon cardigan and Mi Cha was wearing tight blue jeans with a white zip-up. Hyon was dragging her small suitcase of Nari's clothes behind her as she walked. Anthony was sitting on a large rock that was near the shore, but hopped up when he saw Mi Cha come walking down.

"Hey girl." He walked up and gave her a half hug.

"Anthony? What are you doing here?"

"My dad is an officer, remember? He's working with the FBI on this case." Anthony smiled.

"Well, if your dad helps find our little Nari, then you'll have my permission to marry Mi Cha, how's that?" Hyon said with a forced smile.

"Oh I'm sure he'll find her." Anthony smiled again and took Mi Cha's hand in his.

"I brought an extra bag of Nari's stuff…just in case." Hyon said.

Anthony nodded.

"Well, we better get going to the festival." Hyon gestured toward Mi Cha.

"Are you guys staying for the entire thing?"

"Maybe. Why?" Mi Cha replied.

"Oh, uh, I don't know. Just that it gets pretty dark here late at night and I want you to be safe."

"There's going to be tons of people at the festival, I think we'll be fine." Mi Cha smiled then pulled away from Anthony to follow her mother.

"Yeah, right." Anthony said under his breath and turned to ran towards his dad who was calling him over.

7:45 PM

An assembly line of agents and officers in black uniforms walked up to an open field near the line of palm trees at the southern end of the island. The sky was just starting to darken and the stars were beginning to poke out from behind the veil of blue. Amber watched over to her right as the festival came into view, just to the north. It was a large clearing in between the forest of about 3,000 square feet. Strings of pastel colored lights decorated the surrounding trees. Tables were covered with bright pink, yellow, and blue tablecloths. One table had a huge display of wrapped Easter baskets, filled with treats and goodies. Another table was topped with platters of cupcakes, cookies, and other desserts. The longest table was filled with platters of food, including an Easter ham, roasted potatoes, steamed rice, and mixed vegetables. A large container filled with soda cans, water bottles, lemonades, and juices was sitting on the side of the food table, with a stack of colored paper cups beside it. A large rectangular wooden board was placed in the center of the field to act as a dancefloor. Large speakers and a mini DJ booth were set up at one end of the dancefloor. At the very head of the field, a small raised platform sat, with a white wicker chair sitting on top of it. The platform had artificial pink and green grass cluttered over the surface and large plastic eggs scattered around the edges. Not far from the platform sat several games of beanbag toss and ladder ball. To the right of those, there was a huge bin of toys—plastic ducks, fake eggs, coloring books, scented markers, Easter pencils, key chains, and of course, various colored stuffed rabbits.

The first person in line stopped at an area where they would all be out of sight from the people at the festival. Dennis and Amber walked up to the trees first and the other agents and officers followed after. Agents Herman, Clyde, Simon, and Palmer made their way up to Dennis and Amber, followed by Officers Braidy, Philips, and the rest of the team.

"We have exactly 15 minutes until the start of the festival and there are already a lot of people here early. But I want us all at our posts before the second ferry arrives with more. Is everyone in understanding of where they have to go? Agents at the main corners, Officers branched out from them. Clear?"

"If we see anyone are we supposed to detain them?" Officer Braidy spoke out from the group.

"…Do what you can to stop them. And make sure you radio in as soon as possible so that the others can come help."

"And if we find nothing the entire night?"

"Then we begin a search around the area. Zando has to be here. Everything we have—all of our evidence—points to this location, on this night—Easter Sunday at the festival. We *will* find him. Now, everybody to your positions."

8:00 PM

The festival was quickly being filled with people. Young children, older children, parents, grandparents, Aunts, and Uncles were all scattered around the large clearing. Some people made their way right to the tables of food first, others to the dancefloor, and others stood around chatting. Some of the children were dressed in Easter outfits, and some wore plastic bunny masks. The sky was much darker now and the pastel lights lit up the festival in a rainbow of colors.

Music blasted through the speakers as people danced and goofed around on the dancefloor. Some people were dancing with partners, others by themselves spinning on the ground, and others barely moving their arms and legs.

A line was beginning to form in front of the stage, where the kids could take photos with the Easter bunny. The white wicker chair was empty though and they were waiting for his arrival.

At the south end of the island, away from the festival, Dennis, Amber, and Officer Braidy stood in a circle near one of the large palm trees. Their guns were each drawn, but they held them down by their sides.

"This is Lieutenant Fischer, we are all clear here at the South end, over."

"Agent Herman, I'm all clear here at the North west point. Over."

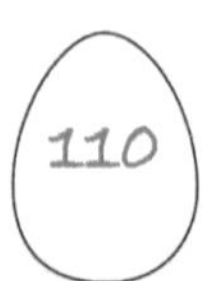

"Clyde, all clear at the North east point. Over."

"Agent Simon, all set at South west. Over."

"Agent Palmer, ready to go here at South East. Over."

"Excellent. Now we all watch and wait. Any problems, you radio in to us immediately. Lieutenant Fischer out."

Dennis lowered his walkie-talkie from his mouth and dropped it into the pocket of his black blazer. The three of them stood there waiting for about fifteen minutes. Dennis paced around a little, but didn't move far from his spot. Amber stood with her back to the sea. The wind brushed up against her long blonde hair and it fluttered slightly in the air. Braidy bit the corner of her lip as she darted her eyes left and right.

"This *is* where Browden said he was going to meet Zando in the letter, right?" Officer Braidy questioned.

"I saw him write it myself. He wrote south end, near the large line of palm trees." Amber replied.

"What makes you guys think he's even here on the island at all?"

"All the evidence points here. This has to be it." Dennis replied.

"Don't you think it's all just a little bit too…clean?"

"Clean?" Amber asked.

"We found a note in Browden's home specifically saying 'go to the festival on Easter Sunday'? To me, that seems a bit too easy. Too simple."

"He couldn't have predicted us finding the note." Dennis said.

"That's not what I'm saying."

"What are you saying then, Officer Braidy?" Amber asked.

"It's just never that clean. You're expecting us to just come here tonight, swoop up Zando from the woods and bring him back to the station tomorrow morning? It's never that clean."

"It's all we have to work with. If you don't like it, then you can leave. We don't need your help. I'm not so sure I trust you yet anyway." Amber raised her voice.

"I've done nothing but help you guys this entire investigation!"

"Amber pointed out something very interesting to me on the ferry ride over here." Dennis began. "The guards who patrol the cell units only have access to the keys for the *cells*. Browden wouldn't have been able to get into the surveillance room to alter the security footage."

"The only person with access to the surveillance room is the chief, which would be *you* Officer Braidy."

"…You're right, Browden wouldn't have had access to the room, but I'm afraid you're mistaken about me." Officer Braidy began. "I'm retiring from the force at the end of the month. Officer Philips is set to become the

new chief, so I had granted him access to the surveillance room a week ago. Philips…Philips was the only one with the keys to that room!"

In the woods behind the photo stage, a man was standing by a tree with one foot inside a white rabbit costume. The rabbit head was laying at the foot of the tree; its eyes were long, with black pupils and its ears were floppy and pink. A big smile was painted on its face, revealing two big buck teeth. The man was struggling to pull the costume over his leg and tripped and fell.

"God! Stupid costume! They really aren't paying me enough for this."

He stood up and balanced himself, then tried to stuff his other leg into the costume.

"Stupid kids want to meet Peter Cottontail." The man whispered under his breath. "Can't just be happy with a damn Easter basket."

He reached out a hand and held onto the tree for support as he pulled the costume over his leg. He finally got it on, then zippered up the front and bent down to grab the head. As he bent down, a branch and some leaves cracked from somewhere behind him. He turned around. It was too dark to see anything, although he could make out the rainbow glow from the festival not far away.

"Hello? Is somebody there?" The man called out and shifted his eyes back and forth.

Another crack of twigs and leaves sounded even closer this time.

"Hello?" The man stepped forward and tumbled over the big rabbit head that was on the ground. He stood up again and turned his back against another nearby tree. "Who's there?"

The cracking sound intensified as the shadow of a man approached. Something shiny on the man's chest reflected some light and the man in the costume could tell that it was some kind of badge. As the shadow drew closer, the man could see its face begin to come into focus; a light beard, dark hair, and hazel green eyes. He was dressed in a police officer uniform.

"It's almost time." The officer spoke. "The children are waiting to see the Easter bunny. What do you say we give them a good show?"

The officer raised something high into the air and hit the man in the costume several times with it. A small squeal escaped his mouth as he winced in pain, but another strong blow by the weapon stopped any sounds that he was making. The officer turned back toward the tree beside him and reached down to pick up the white head of the rabbit costume.

Hyon stood near the dessert table as Mi Cha grabbed a plate and placed a cupcake and few different kinds of cookies on top of it. She also grabbed a juice bottle from the cooler and made her way back to her mother. Hyon motioned her head towards the group of tables and chairs so that Mi Cha could sit down and eat. They sat at the one that was closest to the dessert table.

"You don't want anything to snack on, mom?"

"My stomach is in knots." Hyon said as she crossed her arms over her chest.

"...About Nari?"

"...Do you see Agent Fischer anywhere? I need to tell him something."

"Tell him what?" Mi Cha talked after wiping some white powder from her lips.

"I called the station to request they look into those books that Officer Philips had seen Browden reading—

Hyon was cut off by Anthony who came walking up quickly to their table. A smile was plastered on his face and he gave a slight wave to Mi Cha before pulling out a chair to sit in.

"Happy Easter guys." He said.

"Maybe by the end of the night it'll be happy." Hyon replied.

"That's right, Nari. I'm just glad that Mi Cha was with me and away from home that night. She could've been taken too."

Mi Cha nodded her head. Hyon kept her eyes up and looked around the island for Dennis.

"Easter is always a happy time for me though. I mean, just the magic of it." He turned and talked to Mi Cha as Hyon wasn't paying attention. "The magic of rebirth."

"You mean of Jesus?" Mi Cha sipped at her juice.

"Of anyone. Just the magic of bringing any great person back from the dead."

"It's a little scary."

"Not if it's a great leader who is brought back from the dead. It would depend who it is."

"I guess so." Mi Cha peeled the beige wrapper off of her cupcake.

"Come with me, I want to show you something."

Hyon broke her gaze and turned towards Anthony. "She is staying with me for the night."

Anthony turned back and met her gaze then dropped his head towards his lap. "Okay, I understand. Enjoy those Easter desserts. The night is almost over anyway."

"Well now, I hope everyone is having a great EASTER SUNDAY!" The MC yelled into the microphone at the DJ table. His voice broadcasted through the large speakers. "Let's keep the fun going, shall we? I want all of you kids to get excited because the Easter bunny himself is here TONIGHT!"

A loud uproar of cheers and claps came from the large group of children on the dancefloor and all around the field.

"I know you all want to meet him, and he wants to meet all of you too! You can even get your PICTURE taken with him to keep as a memory of this special night. Now, he's ALMOST ready to come out. He's going to walk out from the woods and take his seat right there on stage. When he does, I want everyone to give a nice round of applause and cheers for him. He's the one to thank for all of your Easter baskets you've found this morning when you woke up. This is his last stop before heading back to his home, so I want you all to make him feel very welcome. It's all because of his special day that we put on this entire festival in the first place. You could almost say, *the party don't start till he walks in,* am I right? Yeah? Any of you kids listen to Kesha before? No? You're probably too young. She was a good like…eh, 7 years ago. Good times, good times. Now you kids are lucky enough to grow up on Miley Cyrus and twerking. Anyway, enough of that. Are you all ready to meet the EASTER BUNNY?!"

Another loud uproar of cheers and hollers erupted from the crowd. The line in front of the stage had become more disoriented and less orderly as time progressed. The children were too anxious to meet the Easter bunny; the man they have to thank for this special night.

"Alright, then put your hands together for the EASTER BUNNY!" The MC yelled and pointed his finger over towards the woods. The green color of the leaves were barely visible and between them there were only shadows of black.

"...He'll be coming out any second now. Maybe we need to cheer a little louder, huh? On three—one, two, three...here comes, THE EASTER BUNNY!"

A soft cracking of some branches sounded, followed by some rustling of leaves, as a white figure came slowly emerging from the trees. The long, droopy ears were hung at the sides of its large, furry head. Its eyes were long ovals with black pupils. A smile was painted on its face, revealing two large buck teeth. Its head turned and glanced at the children and parents in the crowd who were waving and cheering back at him. His glance dropped back to the grass as he slowly walked his way up to the middle of the stage, where the white wicker chair sat waiting for his arrival. He sat in the chair and rested his paws stiffly on the arms. The children all tried pushing their way to the front of the crowd to get closer to the stage.

"Lieutenant Fischer to Officer Philips, do you copy?" Dennis yelled into his radio. "Fischer to Philips!"

"Are you telling us the truth Officer Braidy?" Amber questioned.

"Ask the other officers, they can all confirm that Philips is next in line to become chief."

"If Philips did help assist in Zando's breakout, then what is his goal? Why would he helping us tonight?" Amber replied.

"Maybe he isn't. Maybe he knows that being an officer, we would automatically trust him and he could use our ignorance to his advantage." Braidy said.

"Dennis, if he isn't answering then he probably left his post. If he *is* actually working together with Zando, then leaving his post would leave a spot open in our perimeter for Zando to strike the people at the festival." Amber turned and talked to Dennis.

"That also explains why Zando didn't show up here at the trees like we asked him to in the letter. Philips was a rat. Told Zando about the letter beforehand. Damnit! Alright, let's make our way to the festival right now and make sure everyone is safe!" Dennis said then motioned for Amber and Braidy to follow him.

The three of them ran north, towards the spectrum of pastel colors, until they came to the sets of tables and

chairs. Hyon and Mi Cha were still seated where they had been before. As Dennis came running into view, Hyon lifted her head up first, then stood up quickly. She raised an arm and waved it slightly as she ran up to him.

"Agent Fischer, please, I've been looking for you. Any news? Did you find Zando?"

"Not yet. But I can't talk now, we have a bit of a problem." He replied and continued running forward.

As the three of them were running towards the crowd of people, Dennis' cell phone began to ring and vibrate in his pocket. He answered while keeping his running pace.

"Lieutenant Fischer, hello. This is Agent Karol from headquarters. We have reason to believe that Browden and Zando are not working by themselves."

"You already know about Philips?" Dennis slowed his running pace to talk.

"We got a request from Ms. Park to look into the books that Browden used to read at the station. You all might be in serious danger."

Dennis pulled the phone away from his ear and covered the speaker with his hand. "You two go patrol the festival quick and check out Officer Philips' post to see where he went." He said to Amber and Officer Braidy. The two of them went off as Dennis stayed behind and talked on the phone.

"What do you mean by danger?"

"Our research team found that the books Browden read were about an African tribe called the Vaskas. The Vaskas were a small, violent group of villagers who lived on Blakley Island and were said to perform various rituals as common practice—including kidnap and sacrifice. When their leader and founder, Visaki, was killed by Commander Layton, the tribe was thought to have dissolved and broken up. The recent kidnappings could be a sign that they are back. We also contacted the prison where Zando escaped from and some of the other prisoners say that Zando used to read the same books about the Vaska tribe. Lieutenant, if it's true that the Vaskas are behind this, then I'm afraid that you aren't dealing with only Browden and Zando. You're facing a small tribe of evil, violent people who are determined to stop you from interfering with their ritual plans."

Dennis pulled the phone from his ear as a roar began to burst from the crowd of people in front of the stage. The Easter bunny rose from his chair and pointed one of his big paws towards the dark woods. Something very thin and wooden sprung out from the trees and pierced the body of a person who was standing nearest the stage. The roar grew louder and people began to scream and push away from each other. Another thin piece of wood shot out from the opposite side of the stage and pierced someone else in the chest; they dropped to the ground as the grass around them began to turn red. Multiple arrows shot out at the same time from both sides, striking four people at once. Panic roused through the crowd. Screams and cries grew louder as splashes of blood painted more and more of the grass. Bodies dropped one by one with each piercing arrow.

Amber and Officer Braidy were walking through the woods when the loud screams stopped them.

"What is that?"

"Sounds like its coming from the festival." Braidy said as she turned and faced the direction of the cries. "Let's go!"

The two of them began to run back in the opposite direction, toward the festival area. Officer Braidy was ahead of Amber by a few feet. They each had their guns drawn until Amber lowered hers to call in to her walkie-talkie.

"Dennis, what's going on over there? We hear a lot of screaming."

Some leaves and twigs cracked in the near distance. Amber turned around and saw only blackness and the faint silhouettes of trees. The cracking sounded even closer as she could hear something approaching her. Out of the shadows came something big, with orange fur. It ran up to her from behind. Amber gasped as large paws gripped her arms and torso. She struggled to free her herself from its grip as she began to get dragged into the darkness, further into the woods. She felt helpless being unable to reach for her weapon, or to fight off whatever had grabbed her. Fear was rising inside of her at the unknown of who it was. The fear of the unknown rendered her weaker than she normally would be. The kicks of her legs did nothing but make her feel even more helpless. She tried to dig her heels into the ground to stop the dragging, but it only made her strength weaker. The orange fur was gripped too tightly

around her body and neck for any of her flailing to do any good. She finally let out one loud scream before the big orange paw covered her mouth and dragged her away. Officer Braidy whipped around at the sound of Amber's scream and called out for her, but she was already too deep into the darkness for Braidy to see or hear. She reached down and picked up Amber's radio which had fallen to the ground.

"Amber!" Officer Braidy called out again, but the only response was the screams from the festival up ahead.

She shook her head in confusion as she tried to decide which way she should go—to the festival to see what was happening, or towards the direction where she heard Amber's scream to try to save her. If she went back to the festival then perhaps she could get help from Dennis and go save Amber afterwards, but what if it was too late by that time? Dennis had told her and Amber to stick together, but they didn't plan for one of them to be dragged away. Officer Braidy debated the options in her head for a few seconds, then turned to run towards the direction where Amber was dragged off.

Dennis leaped over and crawled underneath a nearby table and pulled out his walkie-talkie. "AMBER? Amber are you there? It's not safe, some people are shooting arrows out from the trees!"

"Lieutenant Fischer?!" Officer Braidy's voice replied over the walkie talkie.

"Braidy? Where's Amber?"

"She was just grabbed by someone, I don't know, I didn't see. But it was dragging her through the woods. I'm heading in their direction right now. What's happening over there?"

"It's not safe! There are arrows being shot out into the crowd here. We're dealing with a much larger group than we thought. It's the Vaska tribe!"

"Oh my god, what should we do?"

"…I don't know, I don't know! I don't understand how they could have gotten past all of our guards."

"I think I hear some movement up ahead, I'm gonna go help Agent Berns!"

"Braidy, please be careful. It's not safe in the woods at night and we still don't know how many of them there—

"Oh my god, she's dead!"

"What's going on?!"

"She's dead! No no, please no." Static sounded over the radio as Dennis listened in.

"Braidy?! Is it Amber?"

"Officer Sheryl. She's dead. Lying right in the grass here. It's an arrow wound."

"They must have shot down our guards so that they could get to the crowd of people. Damnit!"

"I'm going on forward, I think I can hear Amber's cries. They might have arrows, but I have guns." Officer Braidy said.

"Damnit!" Dennis repeated. "Where's your location?"

"North eastern corner."

"Keep heading in Amber's direction. I'm coming!"

Dennis pocketed the radio and peaked out from underneath the table. Bodies were dropping in piles of blood all throughout the crowd. People were panicking, trying to squeeze through others before they would be the next one hit. The food table had collapsed and the pink tablecloth was covered with blood. The plastic egg decorations snapped and cracked as people stumbled over them. Strands of lights were pulled down from above as people tripped over the cords. Arrows continued to fly out from the trees as Dennis ducked and ran out from his table covering. Someone grabbed his arm and he spun around.

"It's not safe Ms. Park! Take your daughter and leave right now!"

"What about Nari?"

"We were wrong. It's not just Zando. Please, we'll talk later. Take Mi Cha and run towards the shore of the island, stay away from the forest!"

Dennis gave Hyon and Mi Cha a little push and they ran away from the festival and down towards the docks. Dennis ducked below another table and pulled out his cell phone.

"Commander, this is Fischer. We need backup immediately! People are dying here one by one and we don't know who is shooting."

"Shooting?"

"Arrows. It's an entire tribe of people. There's nothing I can do by myself to protect these people. I'm going to look for Amber!"

"Agent Berns is missing?"

"She was taken. Braidy is on their trail. I'm going to help, just send backup immediately!"

Dennis hung up the phone and took off running into a small opening in the trees. His gun was drawn in front of him as he held a flashlight with his opposite hand. A large, circle of light illuminated his path ahead. He ran forwards heading for the north eastern section that Officer Braidy had indicated. His shoes made a steady beat of cracks and slushes over the grass and mud. A twig snapped not far ahead from him.

Dennis pointed his light and gun in the direction of the sound. Another twig snapped, this time in a different location. Dennis spun around again and aimed. A snap came from another direction. Dennis spun. The light went back and forth across the trees until he finally saw something moving—a large silhouette of a rabbit. Dennis pulled the trigger and shot at the silhouette until it stumbled to the ground. Keeping the light steady, Dennis moved closer to the pile of black shadows until he could make out the figure. Bright yellow fur came into view, which was in the shape of a human figure. Long, droopy ears lay facing the grass, and the arms and legs were folded

up as if it had fallen from a building. A small pool of blood seeped out from the stomach where Dennis had shot.

Dennis kept his gun aimed at the body but moved his flashlight around until he saw a bow and arrow at the side of a tree. He gave the yellow costumed figure a little kick with his foot and it rolled over onto its back, revealing the letter **A** marked on its stomach. Dennis lowered his gun and picked up his phone.

"Commander, I killed one of them. He's dressed in a large rabbit costume just like the small stuffed ones that were left at the abduction scenes. This one is marked with an **A**. That's the one who must have taken Ms. Park's daughter."

"Then there must be five of them left."

"*If* that's the entire tribe. There might be five rabbit guys left, but god knows how big their tribe is."

The quiet squirms and squeals sounded not far in the distance. Officer Braidy had her gun drawn and ran quickly to keep up. She could hear the brushing of the leaves against bodies from up ahead and followed as closely as she could without being heard. The path was almost completely dark, except for the spots of moonlight which pierced through open spots in the trees. Braidy slowed her running as soft, orange glowing light made itself

visible from up ahead. The thing dragging Amber had slowed down as well, as it approached what appeared to be a wall made of leaves and twigs. The orange light was sneaking out from behind the open patches in the wall. Officer Braidy moved slowly behind a nearby tree and peaked her head around the side to watch. She could only see their shadowy silhouettes, but one had long droopy ears, and the other one was probably Amber. She was being held by both arms. The rabbit silhouette lifted a paw and knocked it on one of the wooden branches of the door. It uttered something in a language that Braidy could not understand. Shortly after, the door slowly cracked open and left just enough room for the two of them to enter inside. The glowing orange light leaked outside from the crack in the door but seeped back inside when the door was closed. The two silhouettes disappeared behind the wall.

Officer Braidy slowly stepped away from the tree and made her way up to the leave-covered wall. She had her gun pointed down towards the ground as she pressed the side of her head up, against the wall. She could hear movement and quiet muttering in a strange language. She could also hear the soft cries and whimpers from what was probably Amber.

As she was listening, she saw something move in the corner of her eye. As she spun around she saw the long oval eyes of a black furred rabbit. She let out a quick gasp as it lunged at her before she was able to raise her gun.

CHAPTER 6

Amber opened her eyes to the blazing red and orange fire. The glowing light cast shadows across the trees and leaves, as people walked back and forth. Their large, furry faces were lit up with the faint light. As Amber's eyes adjusted, she could make out the colors of the four rabbit costumed people; red, orange, green, and black. She turned her head to the side and saw Officer Braidy sitting next to her, tied up with ropes. She was unconscious.

They were sitting in a small grotto in the woods, surrounded by trees, and barricaded in by a wall of twigs and leaves. Amber noticed the door creak open as another rabbit, white in color, came walking inside. It approached the other four rabbits and began speaking, to which Amber could just faintly hear.

"Where is he?" The white one said.

"Supposed to be not too far from here. Not nearly as far as I was." The orange one replied.

"We cannot complete the ritual without him!"

"I can go look."

"Please do." The white one said then turned to face Amber.

"Boss, wait. Fischer is still out there. What if he…

The white rabbit whipped back around. "Find him please."

"And if he's dead?"

"Then we can go through without him and hope it still works. Two of you go look, safety in numbers."

The orange and green colored rabbits exited the grotto through the barricade door to look for the sixth missing member. The other three paced around the large fire pit in the center.

"Show your faces you monsters!" Amber blurted out after the two had left.

The white rabbit stopped his pacing and turned around slowly to face Amber. The long, oval eyes stared directly into her small round pupils. He stared at her with the wide smile glued onto the mask and began walking towards her. He squatted down and laid one of his paws on Amber's leg and brought his head close to her face. With his free paw he lifted his mask up, over his head, and let it roll down onto the grass below.

"How could you Officer Philips? You're an *Officer*, your job is to help others not harm them!"

"I *am* helping Ms. Berns. I'm helping in the most generous way possible. I'm bringing back a LIFE!"

"You're TAKING the lives of six innocent children!"

"That's unfortunately the only way it could be done Ms. Berns."

"Are they all still alive?"

"And well. We've kept them well for this night."

"And what happens after this night?"

"Are you familiar with the story of Easter, Ms. Berns?" Philips sat on the grass directly in front of Amber and crossed his legs. "Jesus died—was killed for a matter of fact—but came back to life on Easter Sunday. Well, tonight is Easter Sunday, and just like Jesus, *our* lord will rise once again!"

"What kind of lord would condone the killing of innocent children?" Amber began to sweat from the heat of the fire. Her face was glazed in moisture.

"Our lord Visaki; the leader of our tribe. You see, he was killed, five years ago, by people like you. People like you who didn't like his way of living and his beliefs. He was killed! But he will be brought back tonight after everyone gets back. And lucky for you, Ms. Berns, you have a front row seat to witness this great spectacle!"

Hyon was standing by the dock with Mi Cha next to her as the water rolled up and splashed against the rocks. The screams continued to roar as people panicked from the massacre that had just occurred. The entire field was filled with blood and dead bodies. The Easter decorations were all destroyed and splattered with red. The arrows had stopped shooting now, but everyone was struggling to climb over the bodies and get through the crowd of people to leave the area and wait by the shore. Hyon was standing with her arms gripped around her body and watched the people as they ran away from the festival.

"Mom let's call for a boat and get out of here!" Mi Cha cried out.

"I think they stopped shooting."

"We need to leave!"

"I heard Agent Fischer talking. It sounded like Officer Philips was a traitor. He helped Zando escape." Hyon replied.

"Philips? But Anthony…he, he's his son."

"You were out with him the night Nari was taken."

"Yeah…

"So they did it on purpose. Philips told Anthony to take you out so that you wouldn't be home and he can go abduct Nari."

"Mom, I, I didn't know."

"I'm not leaving here without her."

"What are you going to do?"

"I'm going to go look for her."

"Mom, you can't! Please. Let Mr. Fischer and Ms. Berns handle it."

Hyon moved her arms from her body and folded them together in front of her. "I've done nothing this whole time but sit and wait for the police to help; for them

to be my savior. But Nari is *my* daughter. I would give my life to protect her. I'm going to help, I have to!"

"Mom," Mi Cha placed a hand on Hyon's wrist. "I'm your daughter too. I don't want you to get hurt."

"I'm hurt already knowing that Nari is not safe here with me. I want you to stay here on the dock where it's safe and don't move. I'm going to search the woods."

"Mom!"

"Honey, listen to me! Those people stopped firing, so they must have got what they wanted. They won't catch me." Hyon reached a hand over into her back pocket and pulled out a small pistol. "I'll take this with me."

"Were you planning this?" Mi Cha asked when she saw her mom pull out the gun.

"I was planning to get Nari back."

Hyon took a step forward from the dock and onto the grass. "Stay here, I'll be back for you soon." She said before she took off running for the woods.

Dennis ran through the woods following a trail of light footprints and drag marks on the muddy grass below. He ran until he heard the dinging of his cell phone. He stopped behind a nearby tree and put the phone to his ear.

"Lieutenant, this is headquarters. We have some more information on the former leader of the Vaska tribe who was killed. Police were investigating him years ago for reports on religious sacrifice. Several kidnappings were linked to him, and it was found that he was using the

kidnapped people for sacrifice. Police encountered him and shot him dead after he tried to shoot back at them with a bow and arrow."

"Sacrifice…that must mean that they are planning to do the same thing to these children. I think I'm close to their location."

"Do you have backup with you Lieutenant?"

"I told the Commander to send new backup. They haven't arrived yet."

"And what happened to the old backup?"

"…Dead. They were ambushed in the woods." Dennis spoke as he kept a lookout around him.

"I wouldn't go in alone, Lieutenant. Wait for the new backup to arrive."

"I don't want to see any of the children dead. And my partner is out there in danger. I'm going in now." Dennis hung up the phone and slid it into his jacket pocket.

As he stepped away from the tree and onto the small pathway, something smacked the gun out of his hand and wacked him in the stomach. Dennis curled over and fell onto his back. A green colored rabbit was standing over him with a bow in his hand; he had it aimed at Dennis' chest. He placed an arrow on the end and pulled it back until the elastic tightened. Dennis kicked his feet at the rabbit's ankles and rolled over as the arrow shot forward and stuck into the dirt. Dennis got on his feet and grabbed for the rabbit's paw which was holding the bow. He locked it from moving. With his free hand, he gave a hard blow into the green stomach marked with an **R**. The rabbit bent over and clutched its torso as Dennis kicked at its legs until it fell down onto the ground. Dennis searched around with his feet until he found his gun and picked it up into his hands to aim at the blob of green fur. As he placed his finger over the trigger, a red rabbit lunged from behind and grabbed his arms, which jerked his aim in another direction. Dennis pulled and struggled to get free from the grip of the paws. The green rabbit stood up and regained its balance, then went over to help detain Dennis. Dennis pulled his arms away and dealt a blow with his elbow into the red rabbit's chest and spun away from the green one's grip. He fired his weapon—one, two shots. The green rabbit was hit in the chest and stomach.

"Gahh!" Dennis cried out as the red rabbit smacked the side of his head with a large tree branch. The gun dropped from Dennis' hand as he stumbled onto his knees.

Another whack in the head caused Dennis to lay unconscious on the ground. The red rabbit walked over to the green one and cried out as he saw the blood seeping out. He dropped to the ground and touched his fur covered arm. The green **R** on the stomach was becoming stained with deep red.

The red rabbit stood back up once there was no response from the green rabbit. Dennis was dragged by his feet back in the direction of the large grotto with the fire pit.

CHAPTER 7

Voices and chanting rang out not far from Dennis. His eyes were shut, but he could feel the grass underneath him as it pressed against his back. He heard footsteps of people moving about, and he listened to the soft crackling of a nearby fire. He was slowly regaining movement in his arms and legs and tried to lift himself up. The blackness faded from his eyes until he could make out blurry shapes and colors in front of him. Bright orange danced in a blurred triangle shape, pastel orange and red colors in large, tall shapes moved back and forth, and, out of the corner of his vision, lay a blob of green sprawled out on the ground. White and black blurred colors moved over to the blob of green and appeared to bend down to it. The colors merged together as Dennis could hear more voices coming from their direction. A louder voice shouted from much closer. It seemed to come from his left side, as he could not hear anything in his right ear. The louder voice shouted again and he turned his head to see a blurry blob of light yellow dancing in front of his eyes. The voice seemed to be coming from the colored blob.

"Dennis!" He could finally make out what the voice was saying. "Dennis, are you okay?"

As he regained more feeling and movement in his limbs, he realized that his hands and feet were each tied together so that he couldn't move. All he was able to do was sit up from his laying position. As he sat up, the blurriness in his vision began to fade away. The shapes and colors began to sharpen and become more detailed. The blurry orange triangle became the blazing flames of a large fire. The tall red, orange, black, and white shapes became four people in their rabbit costumes. The blob of green on the ground became the rabbit that he had shot earlier. Lastly, the blob of yellow right by his side became the long blonde hair of Amber. He could see her dark green eyes and light pink lips come into focus just a few feet away.

He blinked his eyes a few times then looked down to see the thick ropes binding his hands and feet. Amber was bound the same way. As he looked around the area some more, he then noticed Officer Braidy in the same situation, seated just a few feet away on his opposite side. The white rabbit started walking towards Dennis. As he came closer, Dennis noticed that he wasn't wearing a mask like the others, and immediately recognized his face as Officer Philips. As Philips approached, he kicked Dennis straight in the stomach.

"You killed our brother!" Philips said before kicking once again.

Dennis curled over in pain as Philips kicked for a third time.

"Stop, please!" Amber cried out. "Leave him alone!"

"Stop? Why should I stop when he has killed TWO of us?! He's lucky we don't kill him right now."

"Why don't you?" Dennis spoke out as he lifted his head from his curled position.

Philips turned his head toward Dennis as he spoke. Officer Braidy was watching through half shut eyes, but stayed quiet.

"You got what you wanted. You have all six children for your ritual, you scared everyone away from the island, and you have us three here captured. Why don't you just kills us? What are you waiting for?" Dennis said again.

"We must have four people ready for sacrifice to give strength to our lord after we resurrect him. The six children will be a part of the ritual, which will bring Visaki back to life. Then you all will be used as part of a four person sacrifice to give him full strength."

"Looks like you've miscounted Philips." Officer Braidy finally spoke up. "There's only three of us here."

A slight smirk spread across Philips' face as he motioned a hand towards the red rabbit. "Bring her out."

The red rabbit disappeared into the shadows of the woods then returned, dragging a girl behind him. Her hands and legs were tied up just the same as the others. Her light brown hair slid across the dirt as the rabbit pulled her near Philips.

"Sit her down!"

The rabbit kicked at her legs until she fell to the ground and uttered a cry.

"Mi Cha!" Amber called out.

"Please, help!" Mi Cha said through a face that was red with tears.

"You leave her alone! She's just a young girl!" Dennis yelled at Philips.

"We have children much younger than her that we need for the ritual. Age makes no difference for the four sacrifices."

"Mi Cha, how did they get you? Where is your mother?" Amber asked.

"I found her all alone by the shore of the island. Too bad she wondered a bit too close to the woods." The black rabbit spoke out.

"I know that voice." Dennis replied. "Show yourself Zando!"

The black rabbit stood up and moved towards the group. He raised the paws of his costume to his head and lifted it up. The large, stuffed mask came off and dropped to the ground below. Zando's dark face and deep black eyes were left in place.

"Looks like you found me too late, Mr. Fischer."

The red rabbit dragged Mi Cha to sit her down between Dennis and Amber so that all four of them were lined up in a row. Philips gave a signal to the other rabbits and they all disappeared into the woods.

"No FBI agent is going to stop the Vaskas this time!" Philips cried out.

The other three rabbits emerged from the trees carrying the six children. They were each bound tightly in ropes, and their faces were red with tears and sweat. Amber's face dropped when she locked eyes with Nari for the first time since the start of the investigation. A feeling of helplessness and failure rose in her body as she watched the children being dragged by the three men in rabbit costumes. It was *her* duty to protect and serve; *her* job to find the criminals before any innocent victims are hurt. But here she was, tied up, unable to move, and forced to watch the children whom she was supposed to protect, all suffer. She thought back to her first meeting with Ms. Park. She thought about the promise she had made that she would find Nari and return her safely home. They say that nothing is worse than a broken promise, especially one made to a grieving mother about her kidnapped child. They teach you in law enforcement training never to make promises that you can't keep; that's a very important rule, they say. But Amber had broken that rule, she had *promised* that she would save Nari. It seems to be true after all, nothing is worse than a broken promise.

The path forward was covered in darkness and shadows from the thick trees. Hyon ran through, not being able to see where she was going, but dodging in between the trees. She called out Nari's name every once in a while in hopes that some type of response would at least give her a direction to head in. When nothing responded, she just continued running forward and yelling out until a response would come. Nari had to be out there, Hyon thought.

Something was just telling her that Nari is still alive; some kind of motherly instinct perhaps.

"Nari?! Are you out there? Mommy is going to save you, don't worry!"

She continued forward for a few minutes until she finally found her response. It wasn't the response she was looking for, but still a response nonetheless. It wasn't a cry of help from her daughter, but instead a shining light in the distance; a small dot of glowing orange light. That must be where Nari is, Hyon thought. Even if bad people were to be there, she had her gun with her, so she wasn't afraid. She ran faster as the dot of orange slowly grew larger as she came closer to it. She was still far away but was able to see black dots, which she presumed to be people, moving around near the orange dot. Each of the dots grew in diameter as she ran towards them. She was still unable to see much detail in the objects in front of her, but kept her focus on the colored dots and ran in that direction. She was careful to run in between the trees like a zig zag, so that she wouldn't run into the thick trunks.

Hyon was several hundred feet away from the glowing light when she noticed something move out from behind a tree next to her. It was one of the black dots, except much larger since it was standing right in front of her. It yelled out something and Hyon held her gun out in front of her body with both hands.

"Stop! Don't come any closer!" The shadow of black yelled until it came into sight. It was Anthony, standing right in front of her, with a long arrow pulled back on a bow in his hands. "You're trespassing on tribal grounds!"

The two stood face to face, one pointing a bow and arrow, and the other pointing a gun.

"Ms. Park?" Anthony said and then lessened his pull on the arrow. "Wha-what are you doing here? You shouldn't be here!"

"I came to save my daughter." Hyon replied, still holding her gun in the same position.

Anthony shook his head. "You need to leave now! I don't want to have to shoot this at you!"

"Why are you working for them?"

"Excuse me?"

"You know what your dad is doing is wrong. You don't have to go along with it."

"I'm not going along with anything that I don't believe in."

"I don't know what kind of fucked up religion your tribe believes in, but sacrificing innocent people—children god forbid—is not something someone should 'go along' with!"

Anthony dropped his eyes but kept the arrow held tightly on the bow.

"Anthony, look at me!" Hyon's voice grew louder. "I've known you for a few months now. You've come to the house lots of times, I've been to your house from time to time. I thought I knew what kind of kid you were. I thought you were a great guy; hardworking in school, very polite to me, and I thought you were sweet for how much you seemed to care for Mi Cha."

Anthony's eyes widened when he heard Mi Cha's name.

"You can't fake kindness." Hyon continued. "You can easily fake kind *acts*, but you cannot fake a true kind *character*. I saw that kind character in you. That's why I trusted you so much with my daughter Mi Cha. I thought you were a good boyfriend for her. And I KNOW that deep down you know that everything your father's tribe is doing is wrong. WRONG, I tell you! And you know that Anthony, you know it! If you have ever—ever—sincerely cared about Mi Cha, then help me. Help me save Nari. Help me!"

"I…I do really care about Mi Cha." Anthony finally lowered his bow and arrow and held it towards the ground.

"Anthony, help me please. Is Nari over there by that fire?"

Anthony dropped his eyes once again but nodded his head slowly up and down. "Yeah, she is. Along with the other five children."

"And how many of them are there? Of the guys in rabbit costumes?"

"There were also six of them at first, but two are dead."

"Dead? Were they killed by the FBI?" Hyon began to talk faster and more hysterical.

"Lieutenant Fischer." Anthony mumbled.

"Is he over there now? By the fire?"

"Tied up. Him and his girl partner."

"Okay, listen to me Anthony. Look at me!"

Anthony lifted his eyes to meet Hyon's. A fierce look of drive and determination and compassion were swelling up in her eyes. A look that he was unfamiliar with. It sent a startling chill down his body.

"Will you help me? Please Anthony." Hyon said.

"…Yeah. I'll help. But I'm supposed to be on guard duty, if I walk in there they'll know something is up."

"How many arrows do you have?"

"What?"

"Your bow, get it ready and we'll charge in there together."

"You want me to shoot at them? My dad is there!"

"Aim for the others. I'll go for Philips."

"The time has come!" Philips shouted over the loud cries of the children and the pleas from Dennis, Amber, and Braidy to stop. "Zando, line the children up!"

The other rabbits began to drag the children over near the large fire. Philips took a few steps towards a tree, where a large, ancient looking book was sitting. He picked up the book and began flipping through the musty yellow

pages. He stopped on a page near the middle and walked towards the three who were tied up.

"This ritual," Philips began, "requires the killing of six children from particular regions of the globe. The first letter in the names of their countries spell out the word EASTER." Philips turned to face the black, red, and orange rabbits. "Our Ethiopian is first in line. Followed by Asian."

Dennis, Amber, and Braidy watched them drag Nari to the second place in line. They pushed her down to the ground and she fell onto her back. She laid there as they lined the others up.

"Spanish is next. Ticonderogan, European, and Roman are last in line."

Philips approached the others and stood in front of the fire. The blazing flames danced throughout the grotto and cast soft glows of orange onto the faces of the children. Smoke rose into the air above the fire as the crackling of the wood intensified.

"I will begin reading this right when the first child is thrown into the sacred flames. The rest will be thrown in by intervals of about 30 seconds. Once they all burn up, I will yell out the final reading and our lord Visaki will rise from the ashes on this glorious Easter Sunday. Once again, he will be here to lead this tribe and guide us all on the right path towards virtue and spiritual triumph. And soon after, we will have our revenge on those who murdered him in the first place! People like Mr. Fischer and his female partners. They will pay the price for killing our lord!"

Philips raised the book closer to his eyes and began reading. As Dennis watched Zando reach down to grab the first child, Dennis touched one of his tied-up hands to Ambers. She looked down and noticed a small end of the rope held between his fingers. She looked up and nodded at him, then grabbed the rope end with her two fingers. Her hand could barely move from the binding, but she pulled as hard as she could to try to loosen Dennis' hand tie.

As Philips concluded his speech, he gestured a hand towards Zando, signaling for him to raise the child. Zando lifted the boy with his arms and held him up above his head as he neared the fire. Amber's hand was shaking as she struggled to completely free Dennis from the ropes. Mi Cha was on the ground crying in horror, and Officer Braidy sat helplessly on the side.

Zando was right in front of the fire with the intense heat squeezing his body, when a shot rang out from behind him. One shot, two shots. He dropped the boy down onto the grass and ducked for cover. He began to run towards a nearby tree to hide behind when a large arrow pierced the back of his leg. He fell to the ground and cried out in pain.

Dennis and Amber watched as Hyon and Anthony emerged from the trees firing at the four men. When Dennis' hands were freed from the ropes he quickly reached down to untie Amber's.

When the bullets from Hyon's gun missed Philips, he quickly ran up and smacked the gun out of Hyon's hands. She gasped as he wrapped his arm around her neck and pushed her to the ground. The other two rabbits ran to grab their weapons which were sitting by the trees, towards the front of the grotto.

"Come on, get up. Go!" Dennis pulled Amber up after he freed her hands and legs, and sprinted towards the red rabbit who was bending down to grab a bow and arrow by the side of a tree.

Dennis ran straight toward him and tackled him to the ground. He fell onto his back and his large red-furred mask fell off of his head, revealing a wide eyed, brown face. Dennis pinned his neck to the ground with one hand and reached for the bow and arrow with his other.

The orange rabbit slapped Anthony's bow away as he was trying to reload the arrow, and pushed him hard to the ground. With his large orange paw, he picked up the fallen arrow and loaded it into the bow. He turned around to shoot at Amber who was running in his direction. Amber jumped and dodged his shot, and instead the arrow struck Mi Cha in her ankle. Mi Cha cried out in pain and curled over onto her side as some blood began to seep out from the wound.

Amber charged toward the orange rabbit before he could reload the bow. She gave him a blow to the stomach, but he fought back with an elbow jab into her chest. She flinched backward and tried to restrain his arms but he kicked her in the leg until she fell down onto her back. Her hair nearly touched the fire. The rabbit lifted his leg to deliver another kick, but Amber rolled her body out of the way and lifted herself back up. She delivered a kick of her own into his stomach and he bent over in reflex. Amber tightened her fist and knocked it into the side of the large rabbit head. The mask fell off and dropped onto the ground, revealing a sweaty, bruised pale white face. She delivered another punch to his head which caused him to topple over onto the ground.

Dennis stood up with the bow in his hand and shot an arrow out into the red furry stomach of the man in front of him. The blood that poured out from the shot was an even darker red, and it dripped over the sides of the costume onto the grass below.

Amber then reached down for the bow that she had knocked out of the orange one's hand and shot it at his orange, fur-covered chest. She raised her eyes to see Anthony running off into the nearby woods. When she turned her head around, Dennis was running up towards her. He dropped the empty bow and picked up the small pistol which Hyon had dropped. He raised it towards Philips who was standing ten feet away with his left arm locked around Hyon's neck. He had a sharp arrow in his right hand aimed at her neck.

"You shoot or come any closer this arrow goes right through her neck!" Philips shouted.

"Let her go Philips, your plans are ruined. They're all dead."

"The ritual can still be completed by myself."

"You and I both know that you aren't going to walk out of here freely, so give it up!"

"If I don't walk, then she doesn't walk!" Philips pressed the tip of the arrow tighter against Hyon's neck so that the sharp tip indented her skin. She closed her eyes tightly and squeezed her lips together.

Dennis gave a quick glance to Amber whose eyes were filled with nervousness. She parted her lips and shook her head slightly, as if she didn't know what to do or say.

"What do you want?" Dennis finally said.

"The resurrection of my lord's life! It can only happen on Easter Sunday according to the sacred book, and I will NOT wait another year."

"You're willing to take six lives of innocent children just to bring back the one life of your lord?"

"The lives of the children would not have to be sacrificed if the FBI didn't take the life of our lord in the first place!" Philips gave the arrow a little twist and Hyon gasped at the pressure of the tip on her neck.

"Who was the one who killed him?" Amber finally spoke out.

Philips shifted his eyes to Amber quickly, but kept his focus on Dennis and the gun that was pointed at him.

"Agent Layton, five years ago."

"Layton's the commander now. But he isn't on this island, so if you are seeking revenge, then why are you attacking us and the Park family?" Amber asked.

"I will have my revenge on Layton soon after this."

"It's the end for you, and you know it! Stop talking as if there's any 'after' left for you." Dennis' voice grew angrier.

"You can't stop me without also taking the life of Ms. Park here. If you so much as move a muscle, this

arrow is going straight in her neck. I know you won't do anything to risk her life—especially with her two daughters laying right here in front of her." Philips motioned his head at Mi Cha, who was tied up with blood coming out of her ankle, and Nari, who was tied up and crying by the fire with the other children.

"Dennis may not do anything…but I will!" Anthony emerged from the woods and fired an arrow at the back of Philips. The arrow pierced through his back and protruded out through his stomach. His body twitched and he let go of Hyon's neck. The arrow he was holding dropped to the ground, just as he fell to his knees.

Anthony dropped his bow to the grass and froze like a statue watching the blood pour from Philips' stomach; the splatter from the impact had stained the white fur around it red. Anthony watched in shock as Dennis fired the pistol three times. The bullets each hit Philips until he toppled over, face first onto the ground. Blood crawled out from beneath the white fur of his costume, painting the grass red.

Hyon stumbled to run over towards Nari, but found her balance and darted forward. She picked Nari up in her arms and began loosening the ropes around her small limbs and torso.

"Amber, go help Mi Cha! I'll untie Officer Braidy!" Dennis yelled as he backed away from Philips' dead body.

Amber darted over to Mi Cha, who was crying in pain and holding her ankle. The arrow was still stuck inside her skin.

"Relax, it's going to be okay." Amber said as she grabbed hold of the wooden arrow. "I'm going to pull this out, okay? Just take a deep breath."

Mi Cha nodded and bit her lips as Amber began to pull at the arrow. It slowly slid out of her skin, revealing a large hole in her ankle, where blood rushed out even faster.

"Dennis, I need a cloth or something to tie her wound!" Amber shouted.

"Here." Anthony had run over topless and reached down, holding his white t-shirt in his hand.

"Thank you." Amber took the shirt and wrapped it tightly around Mi Cha's ankle and knotted it up.

"Ahh, that hurts!" Mi Cha cried out.

"It's okay, we'll get you to a hospital when we get back home. That should stop the blood for now. Luckily your ankle bone stopped the arrow from penetrating very far. I know it hurts like hell, but it isn't too bad. You're a strong girl." Amber smiled then began to pull the ropes off of Mi Cha's hands and feet.

Officer Braidy stood up after Dennis freed her from her ropes and gave him a pat on the back. "Great work Lieutenant." She said with a little smile. "Let's get these children freed."

Hyon came walking over to Amber and Mi Cha with Nari in her arms. Nari had stopped crying, but she was scared and her body was shaking. Hyon held her tightly against her body as tears dripped down from her face.

"I told you, I told you Agents Berns. I knew, I knew she was still alive!" Hyon sobbed as Amber stood up and hugged the two of them.

"I always believed it." Amber said through a few tears of her own. "I always believed it, that's why I tried so hard to help you reach her."

"I just can't thank you enough!" Hyon said as she squeezed Amber tighter.

"We have you to thank too! Without you coming out of the woods and causing that distraction, I don't know what Dennis and I could have done. There were too many of them and we had no weapons. You're a hero Ms. Park." Amber wiped a tear from her cheek. "You saved not only your children, but us as well."

Hyon's tears slowed down and she tried to wipe her eyes dry with the back of her hand. "Oh, I'm sure you and Lieutenant Fischer would have figured something out." She tried to force a laugh.

Amber smiled and then went over to help Dennis and Officer Braidy untie the other five children. Mi Cha limped over to her mother and they hugged each other tightly.

"Mi Cha, honey. I can't believe you had to go through this. What happened?"

"I was just looking out at the water and one of them came up from behind me and dragged me away. I was so scared."

"Oh honey, I'm so sorry, I never should have left you alone. It's all my fault."

"You did what you had to do. We're all together now, and everyone is safe." Mi Cha squeezed Hyon and Nari tightly. "That's all that matters."

"Oh, but your ankle." Hyon looked down and noticed the blood stained shirt wrapped around Mi Cha's ankle.

"It's alright. Amber says it isn't that bad, so I just have to get over the pain until we get to the hospital."

Hyon and Mi Cha both turned their heads as Anthony came slowly walking over with his head down. "I…I'm sorry." He muttered.

"Anthony—

"I shouldn't have let this all happen. I could've protected you guys. I *should've*. I'm so sorry."

"You helped us when we needed you." Hyon replied.

Anthony raised his eyes, which were full of tears. His face was beet red. "I shouldn't have let this happen." He repeated.

"Did you know?" Mi Cha asked him.

"Know what?"

"That he was going to kidnap Nari the day we went out to the movies?"

Anthony was silent for a moment and looked back and forth between Mi Cha and Hyon. He wiped the tears from his face and then nodded his head up and down.

"You fucking monster!" Mi Cha yelled and slapped Anthony across the face. A bright red mark appeared where he was hit.

"I didn't know what I could do! He was my father, I…I just didn't know. I never wanted to hurt you! He told me that Nari would be fine, that he just needed her for a ritual."

"Shut up and leave us alone!" Mi Cha yelled and Anthony walked off and sat by himself at the bottom of a tree.

When most of the children were freed from the ropes Dennis stood up and pulled his phone from his pocket and called in to the station.

"Lieutenant! Are you okay? We tried contacting you earlier but there was no answer." Commander Layton spoke over the phone.

"We were in trouble, but everyone is safe now. And good news, we found the kids."

"All of them?"

"All six of them. They're safe. Probably a few bruises and scratches, but they are all okay."

"And Philips?"

"We killed them all. It was a tribe of six, all dressed in different colored rabbit costumes, just like those stuffed ones we have kept in evidence. They're all dead."

"Good. The ferry I sent with backup should be pulling in shortly. Get everyone on that boat and head back. We miss you here at the station."

"Alright, Amber and I miss you too Commander." Dennis smiled at Amber as she watched him talk.

When he hung up the phone, he walked up and placed a hand on Amber's shoulder as she was kneeling down with the children.

"Let's get everybody together and head back to the shore of the island. Layton says the ferry should be arriving shortly."

"What do we do with the bodies?" Officer Braidy walked up from behind.

"The agents on the boat will take care of them. We've done everything we have to do. I think it is best we all just relax now and enjoy our ride home." Dennis smiled, then walked over to Anthony, who was sitting alone under a tree. His face was covered in shadows.

"You were a great help tonight." Dennis said as he approached the tree.

Anthony turned his face towards Dennis for a split second then turned it back down, facing the ground. In that split second Dennis could see the troubled, shocked face of a young teenager from the light the fire casted over his eyes.

"I don't blame you, kid." Dennis said again after he waited for a reply.

"You don't?"

Dennis shook his head. "You didn't really know what was going on, or what to do about it. It must have

been tough. What matters, is that you had a change of heart right when we needed it most."

"Mi Cha doesn't like me anymore."

"She might not. But just know in your heart that you helped. Whether she likes you or not, you helped save her. You helped save all of us. No matter how much everything is troubling you, or how much you regret or feel sorry about, just keep in mind that without your help, we might not all have survived tonight. He could have killed Ms. Park at any second if it wasn't for you. And I promise you, that Mi Cha knows that too." Dennis reached down and patted Anthony's back. "Now come on, we have a boat waiting for us to go home."

Dennis, Amber, Officer Braidy, Hyon, Mi Cha, Nari, and Anthony all stood by the shore of the island with the other five children in front of them. They looked out at the night sky until they saw a few green and red colored lights slowly emerge into view from the water's horizon. The boat came soaring forward as a sign of rescue, a sign of protection, and a sign of relief.

When they were all walking back from the grotto, the adults had tried to shield the children's eyes from the carnage of the festival. Some of the pastel colored lights and fire torches still illuminated the gruesome scene. Dozens of bodies laid sprawled out in the grass, covered in

blood. Broken shards of plastic decorations, ripped open stuffed animals, and smashed up food and desserts were scattered around on top of the bodies. They had all moved past quickly to avoid the horrible scene and get to the shoreline.

As the boat neared the shore, the sound of the roaring motor blasted in everyone's ears. It quieted down as it slowed itself along the dock until it came to a stop. Dennis waved an arm in the direction of the boat, and the group followed him. As they neared it, the large metal door and several FBI agents came running down and met up with Dennis. They exchanged a few words and Dennis pointed a finger towards the clearing where the festival took place. The agents looked and shook their heads, then headed in that direction. Two boat attendants came up the dock next and took the hands of two of the children. They led them up, onto the seats of the boat. Hyon, Nari, and Mi Cha were next to go up, followed by Officer Braidy, who took two children with her—one in each hand. Anthony followed next. Amber was holding the hand of another little girl when she turned to Dennis, who was speaking to one of the agents.

"Are you coming Dennis?"

"I'll be right there. Go ahead." He motioned toward the boat.

Amber walked down the dock with the little girl and took helped her up onto the boat.

"We'll handle everything here, don't worry." The Agent said to Dennis.

"If you need anything, just call me."

“It’s all under control. Commander Layton gave you specific orders to relax and come home.” The Agent smiled.

“Relax? I’m not sure I know what that is.” Dennis smiled back, then turned to walk towards the boat. He placed one hand on the railing then turned back around to the agent. “I’m not sure how many bodies of victims there are, but there should be six bodies of the tribal guys in total. They’re all dead, so you don’t have anything to worry about that. I took care of the hard part, you just clean up my mess.”

“There’s always a mess left over when it’s a dirty job!” The Agent shouted to Dennis as he was halfway onto the boat.

“You got that right!” Dennis shouted back. “Officer Braidy was right, it’s just never that clean.”

CHAPTER 8

11:30 PM

Hyon, Mi Cha, and Nari sat in a row of three seats that were just across the aisle from Dennis and Amber. Hyon was in the middle of her two children, and held each of their hands in her own. Mi Cha was sitting on the seat closet to the aisle. She leaned over to Amber, who was also in the aisle seat, and said thank you for everything that she had done to help her find her sister.

"I made you guys a promise," Amber began to say, "I'm just so glad I was able to keep it." She smiled and gave Mi Cha a little rub on her shoulder.

The other five children sat quietly in two rows of seats at the front of the ferry, with Officer Braidy and the boat attendants keeping watch of them. Their crying had quieted down now and they all sat silently, shaking in their seats. The boat attendants rubbed some of their hands and told them that everything was going to be okay; that pretty soon they would be arriving home and would be able to go back to their families. They told them that they were brave and strong children, and that they were going to have a great life ahead of them.

"I know it was an extremely traumatic experience, but let it strengthen you. You are all very brave for making it through all that." One of the attendants said.

"And if you ever feel scared or need help with anything, just give Officer Braidy a call." Officer Braidy said to the children. "I worked for a whole week straight helping to save you all, so don't be shy to come to me if you're ever in a scary situation. Officer Braidy has your back."

Anthony was sitting alone in a seat by the back end of the ferry. He had his head rested against the railing and his eyes were closed. The sky was almost pitch black, except for the small dots of white stars and the glowing hue from the moon. The water below looked like black tar as the ferry sped across it; it was a lot calmer now than it was earlier in the day. The entire ride back to the docks was about an hour, but it seemed even longer as everyone was anxious to get home. The darkness from outside, and the smooth glide over the water began to make everyone sleepy. The children were the first to fall asleep; some slept still sitting up, while others laid on their sides.

A little over twenty minutes passed and just about everyone aboard the boat fell asleep, except for the two boat attendants, who disappeared into the captain's room, and Dennis and Amber, who were reclining in their seats. Amber had her head rested on Dennis' shoulder, and his arms were wrapped around her body. He planted a kiss onto her forehead and rubbed the back of her head with his hand.

"Were you scared?" Amber whispered quietly to Dennis so that she wouldn't wake anybody else up.

"For the children, yes."

"Didn't you feel so helpless when we were tied up like that? Ugh, that's the worst feeling in the world. Trying and failing isn't nearly as bad as if we had to just sit there and watch people die like that."

"We didn't have to, thankfully. Don't even think about it, because we didn't have to watch anybody die."

"Not any children." Amber said. "But what about all those people at the festival?"

"You didn't have to watch that."

"I saw the carnage afterwards though when we were walking back. How many do you think were killed?"

"Dozens, easily. 30? 40? Could be any number. We'll have to wait and see in the police report once they collect all the bodies."

Amber nodded then lifted her head from Dennis' chest. "Why did they do that? If they just wanted to complete their ritual, why bother killing all those innocent people at the festival?"

"To scare everyone off of the island probably. They knew everyone would try to leave and not come back after that. Everyone except for us. And they wanted revenge."

"Did you hear Philips say that Layton was the one who killed their lord?"

"It was five years ago, I remember when it happened. I was still new on the force and Layton was like my mentor. I was very proud of him for taking that guy out."

"They used to perform human sacrifices?" Amber asked.

"Just like what happened this time." Dennis replied softly. "There were disappearances of people that were linked to the human sacrifices they would perform. Layton found the location where Visaki was staying, and killed him. He found two people that were being kept hostage awaiting sacrifice too."

"And Philips and his gang were a part of that same tribe, and so he tried to bring Visaki back to life using that spell or whatever from the book he had."

"They wanted revenge too for Visaki's death."

"Did they expect Layton to show up with us? Or did they not care who they killed as long as they got revenge on any FBI agents?" Amber asked.

"Who knows what their thinking was, at least they're all dead. That's all I care about."

"…Well, not *all* of them." Amber replied.

"What do you mean?" Dennis sat up further in his seat.

"Browden is still alive at the headquarters."

"Locked up though. He'll pay the price in jail once we transfer him out of holding."

"He wasn't there for the ritual."

"Because we had him detained."

"No, think about it. There were only *six* guys dressed in the rabbit suits for the six children that they captured. Only six. That means that Browden was never meant to be a part of the ritual in the first place." Amber explained.

"So you're saying he planned for us to arrest him?"

"What would his goal be? If he wasn't part of the ritual to bring Visaki back to life, then what would be his job?"

"…Revenge? That's probably why he tried to kill us that night."

"Do you really think he would be stupid enough to break in to our home by smashing a window and not expect us to hear anything?"

"It seems like you're trying to get at something, what is it?" Dennis said, as looked at Amber straight in her eyes.

"Maybe he *wanted* us to catch him and arrest him." Dennis saw Amber's pupils dilate slightly as she said this; something that he had noticed happens whenever she is on to some sort of clue.

"I see that look in your eyes again, so you may be right, but what could he possibly do once he's detained that he couldn't do before?"

"Well…," Amber thought. "He's inside the FBI station, and he wasn't there before."

Dennis laughed softly, but it only sounded like a breath of air since he was trying to keep quiet. "And being at the station helps him do what?"

"…Get closer to the target."

"The target?"

"Commander Layton is the one who killed Visaki."

"So he wants revenge on Layton? That would make sense, but that isn't possible. He's detained."

"…It's a theory." Amber replied and rested her head onto Dennis' shoulder once again.

"And a good one. I'm liking it. But if it's true, then there's a piece that's missing; because Browden can't do anything if he's locked up in the holding room. If you're right, then there must be something that went overlooked or unanswered."

"Well…," Amber sat up again, "We never found out the reason why they left those little stuffed rabbits at the scene of the kidnappings."

"Part of the ritual probably. They had to dress up in those rabbit costumes themselves, so leaving those stuffed ones was probably just another part of it."

"You really believe they *had* to dress up like that for the ritual? I feel like it was just a type of cover-up. Nobody would be suspicious if they saw the Easter Bunny around at the festival. Wearing those costumes was probably how they went unnoticed at the elementary school too."

"Could be a little of both, but anyway, why don't you get some rest? We'll go over any missing details or

questions tomorrow at headquarters." Dennis rubbed Amber's back with his hand as she cuddled her body onto his. She rested her own hand onto the chest of Dennis' jacket, then closed her eyes to rest as the ferry continued sailing back home.

The clicking and buzzing sounds of the computers and phones quieted down as many of the agents left the station for the night. Commander Layton was sitting in his office, working on some paper files that were scattered around his desk. A pair of two agents were walking down the corridor where the interrogation rooms were located. They walked passed one window and saw Browden still sitting inside with his hands tied behind the back of a chair.

"What's he still doing here?" One Agent asked the other.

"Part of Lieutenant Fischer's case." The Agent motioned his head toward Browden behind the window. "The kidnappings one."

"That's right, the one with those six stuffed rabbits that were left at the crime scene. That's some crazy stuff."

"Did you hear what happened? They all went to the Easter Festival on Blakely expecting to find just one more guy named Zando, but apparently there was a whole tribe of them and they started killing the people at the festival."

"What about Lieutenant Fischer and his team?"

"Last I heard they are heading home now on a ferry. I wasn't informed of many other details. But they found the missing children."

"What do we do with this guy now?" The Agent pointed at Browden.

"We're holding him here for the night until he transfers over to the jail tomorrow morning." The Agent pulled out a set of keys and began to fumble through them, until he found the one that fit the interrogation room door. He turned the lock and opened the door. "Come on, we have to bring him to the holding room." The Agent motioned to the other as he made his way inside.

On the floor below, a security guard was heading to the evidence room, carrying the six stuffed rabbits. They were each wrapped in a clear plastic bag that allowed them to be seen from the outside. When he entered the room, he made his way to the first shelf and sat them all up in a row; first the black one, then the yellow, then the orange, red, white, and lastly the green. The letters on their stomach's side by side spelled out the word Easter. The room's shelves were filled with a bunch of other objects wrapped in plastic as evidence; some of them were weapons, others were photographs or pieces of paper with writing on them, and others were belongings of certain victims. They all lined the metal shelves throughout the small room. The security guard turned around to head for the exit, when he heard a small ticking sound coming from behind him. He stopped at the doorway and took a quick look around the room. The sound was coming from directly straight ahead, where he had placed the stuffed rabbits. He looked at them, and their long oval eyes stared back at him. The guard squinted his eyes and walked back up to them. He placed his ear close up to them and heard the ticking sound louder, although still quiet. He grabbed the first black one in his hands and took it out of its bag. He felt around its body and squeezed its arms and legs. When he placed enough pressure around its body he was able to feel something hard inside of it. He placed it once again to his ear and heard the small ticking sound beep faster.

Browden came walking down the hallway on the floor above the evidence room, with the two agents holding his arms. His hands were cuffed behind his back. The Agents pulled at his arms to get him to walk faster, but he resisted and tried to move slowly.

"Come on Browden, don't give us any trouble, you hear?"

"Don't you want to get downstairs to the holding room? There's a nice little bed of metal waiting for you."

"Just a little tired. Don't want to walk that fast." Browden said to the two agents.

"Let's compromise then and walk at medium speed, how's that?"

Browden nodded and continued to walk forward without resistance. They walked out onto the balcony which overlooked the main area of the station, where the many rows of computers and large glass encasement of

Commander Layton's office were located. By that point, many of the workers at the computers have gone home, except for a few who remained at their desk with a little lamp on. The large, white ceiling lights from above were dimmed to a faint yellow.

As the Agents were approaching the staircase at the end of the walkway to bring Browden down to the first floor, a loud boom sound burst out from behind. The entire building shook and vibrated, as several other loud booms burst out afterwards—one after the other—until a total of six went off. A loud siren began to play over the speaker system calling for evacuation of the building. The Agents let go of Browden's arms as pieces of the ceiling began to tumble down. As soon as they let go, Browden sprung around and kicked one of the Agents, causing him to drop to the shaking floor. The other Agent reached into his coat to pull out a gun, but Browden body slammed him against the wall before he was able to do so. The Agent's head smacked the hard concrete of the wall. With the little amount of motion he had in his cuffed hands, Browden reached inside the agent's coat and pulled out his gun and fired a bullet in direct range. As the agent dropped, Browden spun around and shot at the other one who had just stood back up. When both were down, Browden reached into each of their coat pockets until he found the keys for the handcuffs. He slowly pushed the key into the small keyhole the best he could, and turned it with two fingers. The handcuffs unlocked and slid off of his wrists. He picked the agent's gun back up and ran for the staircase up ahead. The railing was vibrating and the stairs were shaking from the huge blasts that had just went off.

Back inside the ferry, Dennis was laying in his seat with his eyes closed. Amber had fallen asleep in his arms. A strong vibration from his cell phone alerted his attention. He sat up quickly and pulled out his phone. An emergency message appeared on the screen. He snuck past Amber without waking her and made his down the end of the aisle to the little enclosed bathroom. After he closed the narrow door, he flicked the light on and dialed a number on his phone.

"This is Fischer, I just got the alert, what's happening at the station?"

"Explosions, Lieutenant! There were six loud explosions, I think they were probably bombs. I made it outside, so I'm safe but I think there are others still inside." One of the receptionists from the headquarters spoke frantically through heavy breaths.

"How many explosions did you say you heard?"

"I think there were six, but I really wasn't counting Lieutenant."

"Did Layton go home or was he still there?"

"He was still there doing work just like a few other agents. Why?"

"Okay, listen to me. The little stuffed rabbits that we had as evidence for this case, there were also six of them. Do you know where they were?"

"Last I know of, they were brought to the evidence room."

"And where did the explosions come from?"

"They came from the back of the building…near the evidence room!"

"Okay, listen, this might sound crazy, but I think those bombs were planted in those six stuffed rabbits. If that's true, then Commander Layton is in danger!"

"Danger? I don't think the explosions were big enough to reach his office, he should be able to leave just fine."

"No, you don't understand. The explosions weren't meant for killing anybody, they were meant as a distraction!"

"A distraction? From what?"

"It's the missing piece of the puzzle!" Dennis said. "The tribe didn't only want to bring Visaki back to life, but they want revenge on the man who killed him! That's what Browden was assigned to do!"

Browden ran past the rows of desks and computers which were now completely empty, as the workers had run off from the explosions. Not far past the desks, sat the large glass encasement which was Commander Layton's office. Browden ran up the five small steps and pulled open the glass door; it almost shattered when it smacked itself against the glass wall. Layton was on the phone but he dropped it to his desk as soon as he saw Browden standing in front of him, with a gun pointed forwards and a look of rage and anger in his eyes.

CHAPTER 9

12:00 AM

"Amber, we have a problem." Dennis whispered as he shook Amber's shoulder. "Come to the bathroom, right now."

Amber hopped up and followed Dennis quietly to the bathroom at the end of the boat. She shut the door behind them as Dennis wiped his hand across his eyes, then uncovered them. His eyes were dark and a little bloodshot and glossy.

"What's the matter?" Amber asked.

Dennis wiped his hand over his mouth then let out a long sigh. "Commander Layton." He finally said.

"What happened?"

"You were right. You were right. I…I wish we thought of this sooner, we could've warned him."

"Of what Dennis?"

"Warned him about Browden."

"Dennis, what happened?"

"He's dead, Amber, he's dead! Browden killed him."

"I don't under—

"You were right, those stuffed rabbits *did* have a purpose. They were stuffed with bombs. The bombs went off and it must have created a distraction for Browden to escape." Dennis shook his head and fought back tears.

"Dennis, I can't—

"He was such a great Commander. And a great friend." Dennis turned his watery eyes to Amber and dropped his body into her arms. Amber rubbed her hand up and down his back and used her other hand to rub the back of his head.

"I can't believe we let this happen." He said, then pulled himself away from her body.

"There's no way we could've known." Amber said in a soft voice. "We were focused on finding the children."

"That's the whole point. I can't believe we let them distract us from their main target like that."

"Those children would be dead right now if we weren't distracted into finding them." Amber reached her hand out and held onto Dennis' arm. "It's not our fault. Don't put this on yourself."

"I only blame myself for overlooking the fact that they wanted revenge on Layton." Dennis shook his head and closed his eyes.

"We didn't even find that information out until it was too late anyway. Those bombs still would've went off."

"We could've warned Layton to leave and stay safe."

"We didn't know he was in trouble!" Amber tightened her grip on Dennis' arm. "I feel just as bad as you do, but let's not blame ourselves. Did we overlook Browden and the stuffed rabbits? Yes, but that's because our priority was on finding the children, and bringing them back safely. And we accomplished that. Our most important job is complete."

Dennis nodded his head slowly and lifted his eyes to lock Amber's gaze. "You're right. But we have one more important job now."

Amber nodded her head in agreement as if she knew what Dennis was about to say.

"The police said he was nowhere in the building after they went in and checked, so he must have escaped. We have to find Browden and bring him to justice."

Glowing light began to filter inside the boat as it approached the docks. Lights from not only the marina, but also from the city in the background, was enough to wake up some of the passengers. Hyon and Mi Cha had woken up, but Nari was still asleep in Hyon's arms. The other five children had woken up from the ferry horn and some began crying, but Officer Braidy tried to calm them down. Dennis watched outside, over the railing, as they began to pull up towards shore. The water had turned from a black tar, to a dark blue, with the shining lights reflected

over the surface. The boat pulled up smoothly to the wooden dock and slowed to a stop, as the large marina building came into view. Dennis and Amber stood up from their seats as soon as the boat halted, and made their way to the front. The boat attendants were already over there, opening up the door.

"If everyone could listen to me for a second please," Dennis began speaking, "It has been reported back to the FBI and the police that we found everyone safe, and were coming back on the ferry right now. For the children, your parents were contacted about this information and they are going to be waiting for you inside the marina. However, please stay with one of us adults until you see your parents. Do not go running off looking for them. Again, stay by our sides until you point out your parents to us."

"We're all set to exit." One of the boat attendants said with a smile.

"Officer Braidy, Amber, and I will walk you guys out, so grab hold of one of our hands." Dennis said.

Everyone stood up in their seats and shuffled their way out into the narrow aisle. Hyon was the first to come walking up, holding Nari in her arms, followed closely behind by Mi Cha. Dennis and Amber were standing just beside the doorway as they came by. A few tears rolled down from Hyon's eyes as she saw the two of them standing there in their black coats and golden badges; like her two superheroes. The tears dripped down onto her mouth, which was curved into a smile.

"Thank you, thank you so much." Hyon said as she dropped into Amber's arms and gave her a hug.

"Thank you!" She repeated as she moved to hug Dennis.

"Hey you." Amber said as Mi Cha reached in for a hug. "Go get that ankle taken care of now."

Mi Cha pulled her head away from Amber's shoulder. "I will. Thank you so much for everything. I really feel like you cared a lot about me. Even the first day when I called and you didn't even know me, you truly cared enough to help the best you could."

"You'll have to stop by our house sometime again." Amber said with a smile. "This time it'll be for fun and not for safety."

"I'll always feel safe when I'm with you." Mi Cha smiled back and then moved over to hug Dennis.

"You're a brave girl." He said to her. "Keep in touch."

Officer Braidy came walking up the aisle next, with the group of children behind her. She held two of them by the hand.

"We make a great team." She said as she passed by Dennis and Amber.

The three other children came walking past and Amber grabbed two of them by their hands. Dennis took the last one in his own hand. Anthony was the last to leave.

They all made their way down the narrow dock, which connected the boat to the marina building. They all

entered through the doorway and into the lobby, where people were swarmed around along the sides of the room. The bright lights shocked their eyes as they had just been in complete darkness for over an hour. Some people with television cameras were set up inside the building to broadcast the news of the returning children. The cameras first caught Hyon walking by, with Nari cuddled in her arms and Mi Cha by her side with their hands locked. Hyon wore a long tan coat which swayed at the bottom as she walked past the crowd of people. She kept her head down as she passed by the cameras, but Mi Cha turned and gave them a glance and flashed a slight smile.

Officer Braidy came walking out next, with two of the children by her side. She was dressed in her dark blue police uniform, but her belt which held her cuffs and gun, was missing. The dark, somber look on the children's faces turned into a bright glow of smiles as their parents came running out from the crowd to greet them. They each were wrapped in their mothers' arms and kissed on the heads by their fathers. The cameras captured the reunion. A few words and smiles were exchanged between Officer Braidy and the parents, before the families broke off into the crowd with their children.

Next to appear through the door, was Amber in her black agent coat and golden badge, holding the hand of a child on each side of her. Two more sets of parents sprung out from the crowd and embraced their child. One mother's face was dripping with tears as she gave Amber a hug before leaving.

The last child came walking out, holding Dennis' hand. Dennis stopped walking and looked out into the crowd of people and waited for some parents to come running out. The cameras watched as the little boy held Dennis' hand and waited. They waited for about a minute and nobody came running up to greet him.

"What's your father's name?" Dennis dropped his head lower and asked the boy.

"Tyreese." The boy said back, softly.

"Is there a Tyreese in the crowd anywhere?" Dennis shouted out. "I have your son with me!"

After a few minutes went by with no response, Dennis walked off to the side of the lobby with the boy. Amber and Officer Braidy were standing by a window at the back wall.

"What's the problem?" Amber asked as Dennis came up to them, still holding the boy's hand.

"We have to find his parents." Dennis replied. "They weren't in the crowd waiting for him."

Amber bent down and smiled at the boy. She grabbed his free hand with her own. "I'm sure they're here somewhere. We'll help you look for them, don't worry. What are their names?"

"I only have a dad." The boy replied.

"He said his father's name is Tyreese. I tried calling out, but there was still no response." Dennis said.

"Tyreese," Amber repeated. "And what's his last name?" She asked the boy.

The boy blinked his eyes a few times, and then said softly, “Browden.”

The Next Day

8:00 AM

Dennis and Amber came walking into the FBI headquarters after they had went home and rested for the night. Yellow police tape was wrapped in front of some of the doors, and the entire side of the building was blocked off for reconstruction. The police guards by the front doors nodded their heads as Dennis and Amber approached, and allowed them to pass inside. They brought the boy with them who had said his father was Browden.

"The elevators are out of order and certain staircases are blocked off for safety reasons." Another guard inside the building said. "The explosions destroyed some of the ceiling, and some of the floorboards in the back are unstable as well."

"Thanks for the warning." Dennis replied to the guard as he made his way to one of the opened staircases with Amber and the boy. They made their way upstairs and took a left down a hallway of offices, until they came to a meeting room.

The room inside was large, with rows of black office chairs around a circular table. There were six other agents sitting at the table before Dennis and Amber took a seat. The young boy hesitated to sit down, so Dennis stood

up and pulled the chair out next to him. The boy finally sat with his head down.

"First, I would like to thank everyone for coming to this emergency meeting." An older lady with gray hair tied up in a bun, and wearing a dark gray skirt, spoke out. "I know this is very short notice, but as you all know, things around here are going to be much different. The bombs last night shocked all of us. Something that dangerous should never had been able to make its way inside this building. This of course raises security concerns, and we are going to have to strengthen our measures of protection to make sure something like this never happens again." The lady stood up and pointed her finger out to the large projection screen on the wall. "Here are some pictures of the aftermath of the explosions. From the police report, it was concluded that the bombs themselves killed only one person, and that was the guard who was inside the evidence room where the bombs were located. The total amount of casualties, however, was four; the guard that I just mentioned, two agents, and of course, Commander Layton."

Everyone at the table dropped their eyes for a second at the mention of Commander Layton's name.

"It's tragic. What we know, is that the bombs came from pieces of evidence from a case that Lieutenant Fischer and Agent Berns have been working on for over a week now—the kidnapped children case." The lady turned in Dennis' direction. "Mr. Fischer, if you could please explain what else we know."

"Sure." Dennis stood up and began speaking. "There was a report of six explosions last night, which

went off one after the other. There were also six pieces of evidence from the case, which were stuffed rabbits in which the kidnappers had left behind—one for each child. We believe that those rabbits had the small bombs planted inside of them and were set to explode the night of Easter Sunday, which would have been right after the Vaska tribe ritual had been completed. Agent Berns and I were of course there on the Island at that time and we helped stop them from completing the ritual. However, the bombs inside the stuffed rabbits went overlooked because we assumed they were only mocking us at first. Tyreese Browden, whom we had in custody here in this building, was also part of the tribe and we believe that his mission to take revenge on Commander Layton for having killed the Vaska tribe leader, Visaki, five years ago. Seeing that the explosions were small, and didn't target any specific person, we believe that they were meant simply as a distraction so that Browden was able to break free and kill Layton. The two agents that Director Hanzel mentioned, as well as Commander Layton, were all killed by gunshot wounds. This indicates that the bombs did not kill them, but that our number one—and our only—suspect, Tyreese Browden, killed the three men. Of course, Browden is nowhere to be found now, so it is clear that he was the killer and has now run off. Our investigation will continue until Browden is captured, and justice for Layton and the two agents is served." Dennis concluded his speech.

"Thank you Lieutenant Fischer." The gray haired Director Hanzel said. "And I see that you brought a boy along with you today. Please tell us the reasoning."

"I'm sure you all saw on the news that Agent Berns and I were able to find the six missing children and bring

them back here safely. Five of them were returned immediately to their parents at the marina, except for this one boy. When we asked him what his father's name was, he replied that it was Tyreese Browden."

Some of the agents around the table opened their mouths and let out a gasp. Director Hanzel leaned in and squinted her eyes.

"I think we can use the boy to help us locate Browden."

"Wow, I can't believe it. But you're right, the boy should help us greatly." Director Hanzel nodded her head. "So that's the story. I want all of you here today to assist Lieutenant Fischer and Agent Berns with this investigation. I want Browden to be caught as quickly as possible, because as the Lieutenant said, justice must be served."

Everyone stood up and pushed their chairs back in and began to leave the meeting room. The six agents were the first to head towards the doors, followed by Dennis, Amber, and the boy.

"Lieutenant Fischer, please stay for a minute. I have something to inform you about."

Dennis stopped and turned toward the Director, then looked at Amber who was standing by him.

"Agent Berns can stay too and listen." Director Hanzel said with a smile.

She waited until the other agents left the room and the door to close before speaking. "So, as you know we no longer have a Commander here. It breaks my heart to say those words, Layton was a dear friend and colleague. I'm sure you feel the same way. But moving forward here is going to be tough unless we have a Commander; someone strong, someone with great leadership, and someone dedicated to helping people and solving investigations. I have seen your work throughout the years, and have been consistently impressed every single time. And I am very impressed yet again with your work on this Easter kidnapping case. When I saw you on TV bringing those children safely off the boat and into the marina, it truly touched my heart how much you care about the people you work to protect. It also touched me how willing you are to put yourself in harm's way to bring justice to the bad guys. And it impressed me that you do so time and time again without failing." Director Hanzel smiled and reached behind her back and pulled something out from her back pants pocket. "So, Mr. Fischer, I am no longer going to call you Lieutenant, because I am promoting you to Commander." She smiled and held out a shiny gold Commander's badge in the palm of her hand.

"This was Layton's badge. I want you to keep it now."

Dennis took the badge and held it up tightly against his chest as a few tears rolled down his face. "Director, I, I don't know what to say. Thank you, thank you so much."

Amber reached her arm over and wrapped it around Dennis' shoulders.

"You're very deserving of it." Director Hanzel said. "I will have a new badge with your name carved in it produced soon. But I want you to keep Layton's badge, not only as a memory, but as a symbol model for the shoes you are about to fill."

"Thank you so much." Dennis repeated.

"There's only one problem now." Director Hanzel replied. "Without you, we no longer have a Lieutenant now." She turned to face Amber and smiled.

"Oh, Director Hanzel, I've only been here for a little over a year, I don't think—

"Nonsense. Time means nothing. I have seen how well you work together with Mr. Fischer, and you have just that same kind of drive and determination that sets you apart from the rest. Now, I'm not going to mandate that you take the position, but I would gladly like if you, Ms. Berns, would be my new Lieutenant?"

Amber turned and looked at Dennis with a big smile on her face, then turned back to Director Hanzel.

"Yes, I'll be the new Lieutenant." She answered, still with a big smile.

10:00 AM

Mi Cha was laying in the hospital bed, with her legs straight out and her back sitting up against the headboard. The lights from above were bright, just like the white walls of the room. Hyon was sitting in a chair by the bedside, with Nari in her lap. A nurse had led them to the room and they were waiting for the doctor to come have a look at Mi Cha's ankle. The pain wasn't too bad the night before when they went home, and the shirt that was wrapped around it stopped any blood from coming out, so they wanted to rest overnight before coming to the hospital. Hyon had asked if she wanted to go as soon as they left the marina, but Mi Cha had said that it only really stings if she stood or walked on it, so she would be able to sleep at home for the night before fixing it. She had said that the main thing she wanted right then was to cuddle up in the safety of the blankets and rest.

After about ten minutes of waiting, Nari stood up from her mother's lap and went exploring around the room, and playing on some of the other chairs. Hyon smiled and watched her play. She was so glad to see Nari coming back to her normal self. The night before, when they had arrived home, Nari was completely shaken and afraid. She wouldn't even eat any food that Hyon tried to feed her, but she eventually had a little bit of soup. They all went right to sleep very soon after, and they all slept together in Hyon's bed. When they woke up, Nari was feeling a little better and she ate toast for breakfast with Mi

Cha. After they ate, they all got ready and drove to the hospital so that the doctor could help Mi Cha's ankle wound heal. She had kept the t-shirt on it all night that Amber had wrapped for her, but by now, the color of it almost all faded to a deep red color from the blood.

"That shirt held up pretty good, huh? It's been soaking up all the blood." Hyon said when she looked at Mi Cha's ankle.

"That's because Amber tied it."

"Such a great woman." Hyon smiled at Mi Cha, then turned her attention back to her ankle. "You know who gave you that shirt in the first place though, right?"

Mi Cha turned her head down and picked at her thumbnail. "Anthony."

Hyon nodded. "You know, he really helped us when we needed him. He saved me. I know you were watching."

"I was."

"I don't blame him for the past; he didn't know what to do. I think what really matters is that he changed his attitude when we really needed him."

"I guess so."

"I'm sure it wasn't easy for him…shooting that arrow at his father like that." Hyon reached out her hand and grabbed Mi Cha's. "But he did it. He did it because he didn't want to see you or I hurt."

"I'm not going to let him be my boyfriend anymore." Mi Cha replied quickly.

"That's not what I'm trying to say."

"Then what?"

"Forgive him. Tell him that you are thankful that he helped save us, and that you would still like to be friends."

"If you're trying to make him feel better, then a friend zone isn't going to help."

"A friend zone is better than a no-zone." Hyon replied. "I think he would be really glad to hear that you don't actually think he's a monster."

Mi Cha dropped her head again, then lifted it back up and nodded. "Yeah, I guess so."

"Once the doctor takes care of your ankle, why don't you give him a call and talk to him."

Mi Cha nodded and before she could say anything else, the doctor entered the room, holding a clipboard between his hands. He walked in with a smile and set the clipboard down on the side of the bed.

"So, Mi Cha Park, how are you doing?" The doctor asked.

"Better." Mi Cha pointed to Nari who was sitting in one of the waiting chairs beside Hyon. "Now that she's back with us, I'm definitely better."

"That's right. I heard about it all on the news." The doctor reached one of his gloved hands down and grabbed Mi Cha's ankle. "If this is the worst injury throughout the whole night, I'd say you all are very lucky."

"We are." Mi Cha and Hyon said, almost at the same time.

"We are!" Nari repeated after.

"I'll have this fixed up for you in no time." The doctor said as he began to untie Anthony's shirt from Mi Cha's wounded ankle.

"Does the new Commander Fischer have any ideas?" Amber asked Dennis.

They were both inside the Commander's office; previously Layton's, but now Dennis was set to take over. Some of the glass wall in the back was shattered from where the bullet had flown out. The shards of glass on the floor were all cleaned up though, so all that was left was the hole in the glass which needed time to get fixed. All of Layton's belongings were cleaned up, including personal files and any picture frames or collectables that he had sitting on the desk. A large pile of FBI related files remained sitting on the desktop in the middle. It was as if Layton had never been there, except for the light stain of red on the gray carpet where his body had dropped from the shot. Dennis slid his shoe across the stained spot and turned to look at the door, then back to the spot on the rug.

"Browden must have come in and shot immediately. I know Layton always kept a firearm in the top drawer of this desk. Probably didn't even have a chance to grab it."

"Where should we start looking for him?"

Dennis turned from the stained rug and gave a little shoulder shrug to Amber. "Could be anywhere. He's had all night to run away."

"We need to find him before he hurts anybody else."

"…He won't."

"What?"

Dennis bent down and rested his hands on the edge of the desk and looked up at Amber. "His mission is completed. He wanted revenge on Layton."

"So you think he's just going to stop now?"

"I think that he has no reason to hurt anybody else. If the six others' jobs were to kidnap the children and perform the ritual, and Browden's job was to kill Layton, then Browden's mission is complete. There's nothing else for him to do."

"But since we stopped the ritual from happening, who knows what Browden might try to do now."

"That's just the thing though—Browden doesn't know that the ritual was stopped. We had him locked in the interrogation room the entire time. He knows that we went to the Island, but he was confident we would fail."

"You're right. So if he thinks that the Vaskas succeeded in completing the ritual, his next move would probably be to return to Blakely Island to meet up with them?"

"That seems most likely to me." Dennis answered.

"You think he would still return there without being certain that they succeeded? What if he doesn't want to risk the chance?"

"Think about it, all the times we had talked to him, we told him we were only planning on finding ONE person—Zando. All along he knew that there were five others waiting to ambush us. There's no way the ritual could have failed in Browden's mind."

"I guess that's true. So we're going to go back to to the island and look for him?"

"Let's not look for him." Dennis said as he stood up straight and folded his arms. "Let's bring him to us this time."

"He's not a dog, he won't come running to us if we offer him a treat."

"Not a dog, but he is a father."

Amber pursed her lips for a second, then parted her mouth open before speaking. "You're not suggesting—

"We'll use the boy to lure him in and catch him then."

"Isn't that a little dangerous for the boy?"

"It's his own father, Amber."

"His own father who was going to let his son be sacrificed for some sick ritual!" Amber snapped back.

"He'll be fine. We won't let anything happen to him. That's all we need him to do is lure Browden in and confuse him enough so that we can easily capture him without a struggle."

"We're just going to arrest him?"

"I don't want to kill him, that's painless. I want him to rot in a jail cell for the rest of his life."

Amber nodded in understanding.

"Which is why we need to use the boy." Dennis said. "If we go out there looking for him, then chances are he's going to put up a fight. He knows those woods a lot better than we do, so he can easily sneak out and attack us. We would have no choice but to shoot him. Using his son will lure him right where we need him and we can capture him without a fight."

"Okay, you're right. When should we do this?"

"He probably started heading back to the Island immediately after he left here last night. We need to go as soon as possible so we can get there before he finds out that Visaki was not brought back to life after all."

"I'll let the others know and request a helicopter for us immediately." Amber said as she headed out of the office.

Mi Cha was sitting in the backseat of her mom's car, next to her sister Nari. Nari was playing with a little toy doll that was sitting in her lap, as Hyon was driving the car back home from the hospital. A fresh, clean bandage was wrapped around Mi Cha's ankle, which the doctor instructed to take off in two days and replace it for a regular household Band-Aid until the wound is completely healed. Mi Cha sat with her elbow against the side of the door and looked out through the window.

"How's the ankle feel now?" Hyon asked from up front.

"Stings a lot worse now after the disinfectant and cleansing stuff was put on."

"A sting is better than an infection though."

"It's not too bad. It hurts more when I walk on it."

"Don't ever walk on it." Hyon smiled and looked at Mi Cha through the rear-view mirror.

"Would be nice." Mi Cha laughed.

Hyon slowed the car as they approached their house, and turned into the driveway. She shifted the gear into park and the three doors opened as the car shut off. Hyon walked up the little stone sidewalk to the front door first and turned the key into the lock. Nari followed, with Mi Cha in the back.

“It’s good to walk into the house all together again.” Hyon said as both of her children walked in after her.

“I’m going to go upstairs to my room and give Anthony a call.” Mi Cha said as she headed for the stairs.

“He’ll be glad to hear from you.” Hyon said as Mi Cha disappeared up the stairs.

She walked into her room and shut the door behind her. The lavender purple bed sheets were still messed up from her sleep and there were clothes scattered here and there around the floor. She straightened some of her bed pillows up against the headboard and threw herself down onto the bed, with her head and shoulders resting on the pillows. She crossed her legs out straight in front of her and pulled her cellphone out from her jeans pocket.

The ringing lasted for about fifteen seconds before Anthony answered, “Mi Cha?”

“Hi, Anthony.”

“I thought you didn’t want to talk to me anymore.”

“I’m still mad at you for not warning us about what was going to happen. For that, I think you’re a big jerk. But, you did help us in the end. And for that, I think that you never truly wanted to see us get hurt.” Mi Cha talked while holding the cellphone up with her shoulder, and playing with her thumbs in front of her.

“I didn’t know what I could have done before. I was too scared. I’m still scared because now my father is gone. But I am SO sorry, Mi Cha.”

"Listen, don't worry about the past. You had a change of heart and helped us all get away from the Island without harm—although this ankle stings like hell."

"I'm sorry." Anthony repeated.

"It could've been much more than just my ankle though if you didn't fire that arrow. So, let's skip the apologies and just move on."

"So…are you saying that we're still—?

"No. I mean, at least for now, no. Look, although I forgive you, I did lose that sense of trust and security in you that I would need in a boyfriend. Let's just stay friends for now."

"And in the future?"

"Let's see how it turns out. Like I said, I don't think you're a 'bad' guy, I just can't see you as my boyfriend anymore. For now."

"You'll still hang out with me?"

"Yes."

"Thank you. I'm glad you can forgive me."

"My mom said you'd be glad, haha."

"She wanted you to forgive me?"

"She explained to me that you really did save us in the end, and that I shouldn't fault you for the past, especially when you didn't really have any control over the situation."

"I was afraid she would hate me even more than you would."

"We can't hate the person who saved us." Mi Cha smiled even though nobody was there to see it.

"I'll try my best to make it up to you—in a friendly way."

"Haha, sounds good Anthony."

"Alrighty…well…thank you so much for the call. I was really worried that I would have nobody to talk to. I'm so shaken up on the inside, just like you and everyone else, the only difference is that I don't have a family to go running back to for support."

Mi Cha thought from the sound of Anthony's voice that he was probably starting to cry. "We'll be here for you."

"Thank you—so much." Anthony replied through sobs.

"I don't want to be too long on the phone, I promised Nari that I would bake some cookies with her today."

"Of course, no problem. Call me later?"

"Sure Anthony." Mi Cha sat up from the pillows and swung her legs over the side of the bed.

"Save some of those cookies for me next time I stop over."

12:00 PM

A team of four agents were gathered on the rooftop of the FBI headquarters building. A large, blue and white helicopter was sitting in the center of the painted circle on the concrete. The rotary wings were spinning slowly as the pilot sat inside with the doors open, waiting for the agents to board.

Dennis and Amber were among the four; Dennis wore a long black blazer with Commander Layton's badge clipped to it. Amber wore a light gray jacket, which went down to her knees. Black, pin striped dress pants covered her legs and ended in leather high heels; her Lieutenant badge had not been engraved with her name yet. She was also holding the hand of Browden's son, as he stood next to her. The other two agents were good friends of Dennis and Amber's, who worked at the headquarters.

The four of them all made their way to the helicopter. Dennis approached it first and stepped up inside, then let his hand out for Amber to grab onto, as she stepped up. Once she was inside, one of the agents lifted the boy up for Amber to grab onto, and she pulled him inside. The two agents followed, and took the seats across from Dennis and Amber. The pilot secured the door closed and gave a thumbs up to everyone on board before he began lifting the helicopter into the air. It rose from the rooftop of the building and curved on its side as it turned towards the opposite direction, before taking off forwards.

"Hey buddy, we never got your name." One of the agents said to the boy.

"Jared." The boy said softly with his head down.

"Well Jared, are you ready to help us out today?"

The boy turned his head up and looked the agent in the eyes, then turned it back down to his feet.

"Does he know what he's supposed to do?" The agent asked Dennis.

"We told him that's all he has to do is sit and wait. We'll walk with him over to the grotto where the ritual was going to take place, then he'll walk out into the middle by himself and wait until Browden shows up. We'll be waiting in the trees until the time is right to run out and catch him." Dennis explained.

"And is there a plan if Browden doesn't show up?" The other agent asked.

"We'll wait there for a few hours if we have to. He'll show up. He has nowhere else to go. And remember, his tribe leader had just been brought back to life. Visaki would be the first person he'd go running to meet. Unfortunately for Browden, he'll be running into us instead."

1:30 PM

The helicopter slowly descended downward onto a small clearing of grass in the southern part of Blakely Island. The leaves on the trees began to rustle and shake, as the wind blew from the spinning blades. As soon as the legs hit the ground, the pilot turned off the engine to be sure that Browden wouldn't hear it if he was already on the island somewhere. Dennis and Amber hopped down from the copter with Jared by their side, followed by the other two agents. The grass was hard and dry from the bright sun of daylight; much different from the soft, wet grass that had been there Easter Sunday.

Dennis talked to the pilot through the little window by his head and told them that they should be back within a few hours. When he met back up with the others, he began to point his hands towards the north eastern direction of the island, where he said the ritual site was located. He then began to walk forwards and lead the group into the woods. It was much easier to see now since the sunlight was filtered in between the leaves of the trees; it was still dense, however, and the walkways were narrow, filled with other small shrubs and sticks poking out here and there. Their shoes lightly crushed some dried leaves and twigs on the ground below as they walked through.

Dennis pointed his finger to the left between the trees as they passed by the field where the festival had taken place. He indicated to the two agents who hadn't been there to see it, where the stage had been set up and where the crowd of people was standing when the shooting began. All that was left in the clearing now was red stained grass, covered with specks of glitter and broken pieces of plastic and stuffing from toys. All of the tables and props and games had been cleaned up, as well as all of the dead bodies had been accounted for.

As they neared the area of the ritual site, Dennis instructed the two agents to draw their weapons and keep them by their sides. He drew his own also and walked close to Amber, who was holding Jared's hand. The wall of twigs and leaves came into view just up ahead. Dennis approached it and placed his ear up to it and signaled for everyone to be quiet.

"I don't hear anything, so Browden must not be here yet. Which is exactly what we want." He said after he heard no noise coming from the other side of the wall. "Step back."

Dennis pulled at a thick branch on the wall as it came opening up towards everybody else. They moved aside and allowed the door to swing open. Large, burnt logs of wood were still sitting in a pile where the fire had been. Some of the grass in a ring around the wood was charred black. The ropes that had been used to tie up Dennis, Amber, Braidy, and Mi Cha were still left where they had been the night before. Round circles of blood stained the grass, where each of the men in rabbit costumes had been shot. Their bodies were also picked up by the police.

"You sure this is the right plan?" Amber asked Dennis as they approached the center of the grotto.

"We'll have the boy go out and stand in the middle there, and we'll go hide in the woods on the left and wait until Browden shows up."

"Isn't there a way we can do this without endangering Jared?"

"Browden will most likely arrive with a weapon and he'll be on lookout. Without causing any distraction or confusion, there would be no way we could just run out and grab him without him shooting at us."

"We could just shoot him from here."

"We're not doing that!" Dennis snapped back. "I told you already, I want that man locked up for life."

Amber nodded and then let go of Jared's hand, after giving him a little push forwards. She motioned her hand forward and directed him to stand in the middle of the clearing and wait there for his father. She instructed him not to move or say anything when he showed up—just wait and let them take care of the rest. Jared slowly, and cautiously, moved forward until he came to the middle of the clearing and stopped. Dennis, Amber, and the two agents have already started to make their way behind the trees on the right side of where Jared was standing.

Dennis led the group a few feet into the woods and up to the area where they could look straight out at Jared standing there. Jared stood in place, but turned his head and body around left and right. His arms swung at his sides.

"How long do you think it'll take for Browden to show up?"

"I'm sure he left as soon as he was finished at the headquarters. So he's probably already on the island. He just has to come to this location now."

The four of them stood motionless and quiet behind the trees with their guns held between their hands. They watched out between the tree trunks as Jared stood in the middle of the field, and as the sky began to cover with gray clouds. They waited in the same position for about twenty minutes before they saw the outline of a person come walking from far away.

"That's him." Dennis nudged Amber with his elbow. "Get ready."

They watched as the outline grew bigger and more detailed as it came closer to their location. The long, black lines turned into thick legs, and the round dot grew into the torso of a body. The arms seemed to be lifted by its sides, as if it were holding something between them. The man's dark eyes and stern face finally came into view, as he was only a few yards away. His attention was not on Jared however, and instead, was turned towards the trees where the group of agents were hiding.

"Is he looking at us?" Amber whispered.

"He can't see us." Dennis answered.

As the man came up even closer, his facial features were now apparent, as well as his clothing, and the item in his hands. Dennis noticed that he was wearing rugged black shorts and a ripped white t shirt. He was holding a long bow and arrow between his hands, which was pointed towards the ground. He walked up and turned his head at the sight of his boy standing there in the field. He slowed

his walk and then began to turn his head left and right at the trees around him. He turned his gaze forward at the burnt pile of sticks and the patches of red blood in the grass, where the ritual was supposed to have taken place.

The cracking of a twig turned Browden's gaze towards the trees, where the agents were hiding behind.

"Who made that noise?" Dennis turned around and whispered to the other three. They all shook their heads in response.

The cracking sounded once again, as another man appeared between the trees just a few feet away. He was wearing a suit of black fur and his right leg was torn with a large wound from an arrow.

"Get down! Get down! It's Zando!" Dennis shouted as an arrow came flying out in his direction.

He and Amber ducked quickly enough, but the arrow flew over their heads and hit one of the other agents in the shoulder.

"Watch out!" Dennis shouted again as Zando began to fire more arrows in their direction.

Amber stood up and straightened her body tightly behind the trunk of a tree to use as a shield. Dennis was ducked underneath a large shrub, and the other two dodged the arrows as they ran for cover. When Amber peaked her head around the side of the tree trunk, an arrow went flying right past her face; she quickly turned her head back around. Dennis pointed his gun between the leaves of the shrub and began to fire bullets in Zando's direction. He could see only the black, fur covered legs of Zando through the shrub—the bullets didn't seem to hit him.

Amber peaked her head around the tree trunk in the other direction and noticed Browden running towards Jared and grabbing him in his arms.

"Dennis! Browden just took Jared!"

Dennis stood up on his knees and peered around the side of the shrub. He shot his gun three more times at Zando's direction; one of the bullets hit him in the leg. Zando let out a cry and dropped to his knees. Dennis then aimed his gun towards the other direction and began to shoot towards Browden, who was running away with Jared in his arms.

"Don't! You might hit the boy!" Amber said to Dennis as he was firing.

"Let's go then!" Dennis pulled at Amber's arm as he ran out from his hiding spot. He fired his gun three more times at Zando who was already on his knees. The bullets pierced his legs until he finally tumbled over onto his stomach, as blood seeped out from underneath.

"Commander Fisher, Agent Whyman has been hit!" The other agent called out from a few feet away.

"Bring him back to the helicopter and get him taken care of! Amber and I are going for Browden!" Dennis shouted back as he began to run out of the woods and in the direction where Browden was headed.

Amber followed closely behind as the ground began to slant upward in a hill. She ran with her gun drawn, pointed towards the grass. Browden was just up

ahead, towards the top of the hill, where it appeared as if he had slowed down.

"Come on, he's at the edge of the island!" Dennis called back to Amber.

They picked up their pace and jogged up the steep hill, until it finally leveled out flat. They pointed their guns out straight as they saw Browden standing at the cliff edge, just up ahead. He was standing there, faced towards them, and holding Jared over the edge of the cliff, above the water.

"Let him go, Browden!" Amber shouted.

"It's never too late for a sacrifice." Browden said.

"The other five children are safe in their homes. The ritual can't be completed with only one child."

"Alive or dead, our lord Visaki must still be honored with sacrifice."

"He's your own son, goddamnit! How sick are you?!"

"It proves a much greater honor if I am willing to sacrifice my own son for the lord Visaki."

"If you think you're going to walk out of here freely for that sacrifice to even make a difference on your life, you better think again!" Dennis shouted.

"What, are you going to shoot me?" Browden replied. "You shoot me, then the boy drops thirty feet into the rocky water below."

"Just let him go Browden!" Dennis took a few steps forward, but stopped when Browden let one of his hands go from the boy. Jared dangled in the air and flailed his feet back and forth.

"Come any closer and he drops."

"What do you want Browden?" Amber asked.

"A sacrifice!" Browden shouted back. "But I see that you two really care about my boy here, so I'll make you a deal. I'll let him go, if I can push one of you two off the cliff instead."

"That's not going to happ—

Dennis waved a hand back at Amber. "Okay," he said, "I'll do it."

"Dennis, what are you—

"Perfect." Browden said. "I got my revenge on Layton for killing my lord, now I'll get my revenge on *you* for killing my tribal members."

Dennis began to step forward but Browden put up his hand.

"Ah uh, don't take one step closer until both of you drop your weapons."

Dennis turned back towards Amber and nodded his head. She reluctantly lowered her gun to the ground and let it drop. Dennis did the same, and kicked it backwards away from him.

"Give Amber the boy." Dennis said.

"I'm sorry, but I don't trust you. You're going to have to go first before I give her my boy."

Dennis turned his head back towards Amber and looked at her sullen eyes. Her mouth was parted in a look of worry and nerves. He gave a quick nod of his head towards her, before he turned around and ran forwards, towards the cliff's edge.

CHAPTER 10

Amber watched in horror as Dennis took off running towards the edge of the cliff. Browden's eyes widened as he saw Dennis come jolting forward. Dennis lifted his hands out in front of him and slammed into Browden's chest. He fell backward onto one foot, until his body was tipping towards the water below. Dennis lunged forward and grabbed Jared's free hand, when his foot slipped off of the grass. Dennis came tumbling down, but gripped the side of the ledge with his left hand, while his right hand held Jared in the air. Browden had lost his grip on Jared and went falling towards the rocky water with his back first. Dennis watched below him as Browden's arms and legs swayed back and forth in panic, as his body went soaring downward. A loud scream escaped from Browden's throat as his body smacked into the rocks. Splats of red blood painted the white stones, as the body began to sink into the water. Dennis waited until Browden was completely submerged before he yelled to Amber for help. When he lifted his eyes, she was already standing there on the cliff looking down at him.

"I don't know if I can pull you both up!" She said as she began to pull at Dennis' arm.

Dennis pulled with all of his strength, but with his other hand weighed down by Jared, he wasn't able to lift himself.

"The harder I pull I can feel my grip slipping!"

"Can you hold until I tell McDaniel to come help you?"

"Forget that! I don't know how long I can hold and that could take a while, the helicopter is on the other end of the island."

Jared began to cry as his body was blowing in the wind, as if he were a loose branch on a tree. Dennis' hand was slowly slipping away from its grip on the cliff's edge.

"What do I do Dennis?!"

"Find something—something I can grab onto so that you can pull us up with it."

"There's nothing around here except trees!" Amber said as she looked to the left and right frantically.

"A vine, a long branch, anything! Hurry!"

Amber let go of Dennis' arm and ran back towards the trees. The ground was covered with old, dried leaves and tons of broken twigs. She looked around, trying to find any kind of branch that was still intact or some kind of long vine. She walked through the trees for about a minute until she saw something thick and green beneath some leaves in the grass. She lifted it, and began to pull. As she pulled, she realized that it wasn't a vine, but instead felt like some sort of soft wire. Unlit colored bulbs began to appear on the wire as she pulled more—some of them were broken, while others were still intact. She pulled about forty feet of lights that had been used to decorate the island for the Easter festival, then quickly wound them up into a ball to bring back to Dennis.

As she appeared out of the trees, she could see the small tips of his fingers gripping tightly on the side of the cliff. As she approached him more, she could see the black top of his hair and part of his forehead.

"I found a little Easter egg in the woods." She said as she raised the ball of lights so that he could see them.

"That should work. Throw the end of them down to Jared and pull him up first. It'll be easier for me if I can use both hands."

Amber unwound them and threw the end of the light strand down towards Jared, who was hanging helplessly in Dennis' grip.

"Jared, I want you to grab hold of the lights and let go of Dennis, understand?" Amber called down to him from above.

Jared looked back up at her with tears in his eyes, but gave a little nod of his head. With his free hand, he grabbed hold of the lights until he had a good grip on them, then slowly let go of Dennis with his other hand. As he did that, the wind carried his body away from Dennis a few feet and he let out a scream. His body was tossed against the side of the rocky cliff.

"Don't let go! Do not let go! I'm pulling you up!" Amber shouted over the boy's cries, as she pulled at her end of the lights until his body began to slowly rise up. She pulled until his stomach was sprawled across the flat surface of the ground, then ran over and helped him to his feet.

Dennis swung his free hand up, onto the side of the cliff, so that he was now holding himself up with both hands. Amber ran over and handed him the end of the light strand. He gripped his hand around the thick green plug that was at the end of the strand and let go of the cliff. Amber dug her shoes into the dirt, just trying to hold Dennis' weight.

"Pull Amber, pull!"

Amber pulled hard and Dennis began to rise, until the green plug at the end of the strand ripped off from the pressure of his hand. His grip slipped off of the lights and he began to fall down, his body scraped against the side of the cliff.

As he fell, he kept trying to push his hand up against the rocky wall to find some kind of ledge that he could grab hold of. He scraped his shoes against the rocky wall to slow his speed and finally found a small cut in the rocks where he grabbed hold of. He was dangling at about thirty feet below Amber on the side of the cliff.

He turned his gaze up towards Amber, whose head was peering over the edge, although her face was blocked in shadows by the sun. He watched as the green strand of lights came easing its way down. He yanked on it with his free hand and felt it to be secure, before he let go of the cliff. Both of his hands were on the lights as he tried to place his feet flat against the surface of the cliff, as if to hike up it. Amber pulled at the lights as hard as she could from above, while Dennis held tightly onto the opposite end and tried to lessen some of his weight by digging into the cliffside with his feet. He rose inch by inch, until the top of his head came to the cliff's edge. He could see that

Amber had the strand of lights wrapped a few times around her wrists, as she pulled tightly. He even noticed that Jared was standing behind her, pulling at the lights as well.

With a few more hard tugs, Dennis was high enough to place his feet firmly onto the surface and stand up. He dropped his end of the lights as Amber came running towards him. She fell into his arms as he squeezed her body against his and rubbed the back of her head.

"When that plug broke I thought I was going to lose you." She spoke into his ear as her head was rested on his shoulder.

"You're never going to lose me." He said and hugged her tighter.

Amber loosened her grip and pulled away from him to look at his torn jacket and scuffed face and neck.

"Are you okay?" She asked while touching his cheek with her thumb.

"Just a few scrapes." He replied. "Not like him." Dennis turned and waved his hand towards the bloody rocks below. "I would have liked to see him rot away in jail for the rest of his life, but I guess we can call this a sacrifice for our lord and Commander, Layton."

Amber smiled and nodded before wrapping her arm once again around Dennis' shoulders.

"Hey!" A voice yelled out from behind. "Hey, are you guys okay? I heard screaming, so came running as fast as I could." Agent McDaniel came running up the hill towards the three of them. He stopped and gave a look at

Jared, who was standing there silently, then looked at Dennis and Amber. "Where's Browden?"

Dennis pointed his finger over the edge of the cliff. "That's all of them. They're all dead now."

"Not all." McDaniel replied. "Zando is still alive. When I came back, I saw him lying in a pile of blood, but only his legs were hit. We got him bandaged up and he's detained in the copter."

Dennis let out a small smirk. "Well, at least one of them will rot in a jail cell."

Agent McDaniel smiled and took Jared's hand as the four of them walked back down the hill, towards the helicopter, to fly back home.

4:30 PM

Dennis and Amber were back in the conference room at FBI headquarters, talking to Director Hanzel and several other agents. They were discussing some final details and going over their reports in order to create closure for the investigation. Dennis reached into his briefcase and pulled out a yellow folder of police files regarding the victims from the Easter festival.

"Police reports show a total of 36 bodies were found at the site of the festival. 30 of whom were dead, 6 critically injured and were brought back to be treated at hospitals in the city. A total of six members of the tribe were lawfully killed in self-defense by members of our team. Zando was shot several times in the leg, but was brought back here to be held at headquarters until the police transfer him to a jail cell. All six of the kidnapped children were found and returned safely home, with the exception of a young boy named Jared, who was the son of Tyreese Browden. Browden was killed by myself, in an effort to protect the young boy. Jared Browden will now be placed in foster care by a family who is willing to take care and support him the way he deserves to be. With all that information, Lieutenant Berns and I are highly confident that there is no further investigation, nor any more pursuits to be made, and that this case can officially be closed at this time." Dennis spoke, then closed the folder and filed it back into his briefcase.

Director Hanzel and the other agents smiled and applauded.

"Huge congratulations Commander Fischer. Excellent work—the both of you." Hanzel said as she made her way around the table and shook the hands of Dennis and Amber. "And a thanks to everyone here who helped with the behind the scenes work on the case. I know it wasn't easy, but you all prevailed strongly, just as I expected. Commander Layton would be very proud. And I know somewhere up above, he's applauding you all as well."

Hanzel walked back to the head of the table and lifted her purse from the ground. She dug her hand into it until she pulled out two shiny, gold badges. "Here you are Mr. Fischer, just got finished today." She smiled as she handed him his official Commander's badge. The gold plating was new and fresh, without any smudge or scratches.

Dennis peered his head over above the surface of the badge and saw his reflection in the gold, as crisp as day. He picked it up from the director's hands and held it in his own. He rubbed his thumb over the engraved text at the bottom of it that read *Commander Dennis Fischer, FBI.*

"It's an honor." He said as he sealed it away inside his jacket pocket.

"And yours as well, Ms. Berns." Director Hanzel reached out her other hand and handed Amber her official Lieutenant badge, engraved with her name, *Lieutenant Amber Berns, FBI.*

"Wow, this thing is so big. It might take some getting used to haha." Amber smiled as she felt the size and weight of the new badge compared to her old, standard badge.

"The bigger it is, the more powerful it makes you." Director Hanzel replied.

"How big is yours, director?"

Hanzel's mouth wrinkled into a smile as she made her way back to her chair. "So big I don't even need to wear one." She replied with a laugh.

As the group of agents left the conference room to go home, Dennis and Amber took a left turn and walked down the hall to where Zando was being held in detainment. Dennis swiped his key card through the scanner and opened the door. Zando was sitting in the room alone with his head down, and arms tied into handcuffs behind his back.

"Time to go." Dennis said as he and Amber lifted him from his seat and walked him out of the room. They made their way outside the building, where a police car from the local station was waiting by the sidewalk. A woman in a dark blue police uniform and dirty blond hair leaned up against the car, with her arms crossed in front of her chest. She pulled her sunglasses off and stood up straight as Dennis and Amber approached her.

"There's the new lieutenant and commander!" She said to them.

"Officer Braidy, great to see you again!" Amber replied.

"You still working at the station, I thought you were going to retire?" Dennis asked.

"Retire and let one of those goofballs at the station become the new chief? Hah, not happening anymore. I don't trust a single one of em after everything that happened with Browden and Philips."

"Hopefully we'll be working together more for future cases then."

"We can handle anything now." Officer Braidy smiled, then turned her attention toward Zando, who was standing with his head towards the ground.

"So you're the last one left, huh?" She said to him. "I think this goes to show that you cannot hide from the law. Ain't nobody there anymore that's going to help you break out this time, you hear?"

She pulled the back door of the cop car open, as Dennis pushed him inside.

"I'll set him up with a nice little cell all by himself, where he can sit for the rest of his life." Officer Braidy said, before closing the door. "So, what happened with that bastard Browden?"

"We chased him back to the island, where we figured he was going to head next. Only, we didn't realize that Zando was still alive, so he attacked us while we were waiting in the woods. Long story short, Browden ran with Jared to the edge of the island and was going to throw him over the cliff, so I tossed his ass over instead." Dennis explained.

"It's crazy to think how sick some people can be." Braidy shook her head. "I'm just glad they all got what they deserved in the end. I always tell myself that people get what they deserve in life—for the most part that is. I think I deserve a pretty hefty raise after this, but we'll see what the city thinks of that, haha." She said and then went over and gave both Dennis and Amber a light tap on their shoulders.

"Have a good night you two." She said finally, before hopping back into her police car, and driving off, back to the station.

"You ready to go have a good night?" Dennis said softly as he turned his head towards Amber.

"…Are you?" She smiled then turned towards the direction of the parking lot for their car.

Dennis parked the car in the driveway of his house and shut of the lights. The sun was just starting to set and it created a light pink and orange hue across the sky. Dennis and Amber emerged from the vehicle, and began to walk up the stone sidewalk, towards the front door. Dennis stopped at the first step and turned around and pointed up towards the pastel colored sky.

"Look," he said, "Easter colors."

“Don’t remind me.” Amber smiled and made her way up to the door first. She turned a key into the lock and walked inside the cool, air conditioned house. She flicked on some lights as she took off her coat and hung it on one of the hooks beside the door.

Dennis did the same after shutting the door behind him, but took one of the gold badges out from the coat pocket—Commander Layton’s.

“What are you going to do with that?” Amber asked.

“Keep it somewhere nice. I can’t actually use it since my name isn’t on it.”

Dennis walked forward through the foyer and into the kitchen, where he walked up to the edge of the table. He ran his fingers and thumb over the engravings once again and tilted it back and forth as the light shined across the surface. He gently set it down on the tabletop.

“We have nicer places to keep it than the kitchen table.” Amber said with a smile as she walked up from behind and wrapped her arms around Dennis’ stomach.

“I’m not going to leave it here.” He turned his head until he could feel Amber’s, which was resting on his shoulder. “We can keep it on a shelf in our bedroom.”

“What should I cook for dinner?”

“Let’s order something from someplace. I think we both deserve a little break.” Dennis replied as he turned around and hugged Amber back.

“I can second that notion.” She crinkled her face into a smile and then leaned in for a kiss. She pressed her lips up against Dennis’, as he rubbed his hands up and down her back. He touched the thin fabric of her shirt and felt the small bump of her bra underneath. He held her tighter against his body as they kissed.

“Haven’t had much time for this in a while.” Dennis said as he moved his face away from Amber’s slightly.

“We do now.”

They both walked out of the kitchen while they held each other, and made their way upstairs to their bedroom. Amber walked backwards, until she felt the press of the bed’s mattress against the backs of her legs, then laid down. Dennis pulled at the collar of his shirt until it came unbuttoned, then continued to unbutton the rest. He pulled it off of his arms and threw it against the wall of the bedroom. Amber sat up and pulled at the sides of her blouse until it came off of her arms; she let it fall down onto the bed right next to her.

Dennis kicked off his shoes then lifted one knee up, onto the bed, next to Amber’s leg. He lowered his body until his chest felt the soft fabric of Amber’s bra and then moved his lips up to meet hers. With one hand, he ran his fingers through her lush, blonde hair, and with his other hand, he gripped the side of her stomach.

Amber began to reach her hand down to Dennis’ belt and unhooked it from his pants. She unzipped his pants and then pulled them down, until he was in only his boxer shorts. Dennis lifted himself up to his knees then

began to pull at Amber's pants until they came off and revealed the see-through fabric of her underwear. She lifted her legs up and wrapped them around Dennis' body as he pressed himself against her once again with another kiss. His hands slid down the soft skin of her stomach until he came to the fabric of her underwear, where he reached his hand down inside to pull off. Amber touched her hands down Dennis' chest and stomach, and then began to touch over the top of his boxer shorts.

"How's that, Commander?" Amber said as she continued to rub over his shorts.

"Feels even better if you take my shorts off first."

Amber pulled Dennis' boxer shorts down, just as he pulled her underwear off of her legs, and unhooked her bra. He pressed his body down on top of her once again as his lips went to her neck this time.

The Next Week

7:00 AM

"Mom, how could you do this to me?!" Mi Cha yelled down from her upstairs bedroom. "They're gonna kill me!"

Hyon was in the kitchen, with a package of sliced turkey, mayonnaise, and bread sitting on the counter top in front of her. Two brown, paper lunch bags were beside her.

"You're gonna be in college next year, so you better learn to wake up on your own without your mother." She yelled back.

"I'm going to be so late! I lost a whole half an hour because you didn't wake me up."

"Don't spend so much time on your hair and makeup, and you'll easily make it to school on time."

"Ugh, this is so stupid!" Mi Cha said as she sat at a vanity table in her room, with a small brush held up to her eyes. She moved the brush slowly across her eyelids and painted a thin black liner on them, and ended the corners in a small wing. After she placed the brush back into its container, she picked up a large brush and began to run it through her light brown hair. Her hair was completely straightened, and ran all the way down to her chest. She

wore a thin, black shirt that was cut off to show her belly button, and had sleeves that went halfway down her arms. Skinny blue jeans, with a few rips on the front of them for design, covered her legs.

Mi Cha hurried as she tried to pack everything into her backpack, since she was running thirty minutes later than usual for school. Easter break had just ended, so she now had less than two months to go to finish out her senior year of high school, and move on to college in the fall. She bolted out of her bedroom doorway after she stuffed the last stack of papers into her bag. Her shoes clapped against the wooden stairs as she ran down them.

"Well, good to see your ankle isn't bothering you anymore." Hyon said as she watched Mi Cha bolt down from upstairs.

"Where is my lunch?"

Hyon lifted up one of the brown paper bags and Mi Cha scooped it into her hands and headed for the door.

"Nari is so lucky that her school starts an hour later than mine."

"One day she'll be going to school the same time that you are now." Hyon replied. "But anyway, I got a call from Amber Berns this morning and they invited us all to have dinner with them tonight. So come home right when you get out of class, and make sure you get all your homework done before we have to leave."

"Sounds good. I can't wait to see them again—for just a friendly visit this time." Mi Cha said, then pulled the door open.

"Have a good day honey, and drive safe. Don't speed just because you're running a little bit late!"

Mi Cha stepped outside and let the bright, warm sun shine on her face, before walking to the driveway. She opened her car door and threw her backpack over to the passenger's seat before she seated herself. After she started the car, she clicked the Bluetooth button on her cellphone and connected it to the car's stereo to play her favorite music from CL.

She drove the car through the quiet morning streets as fast as she could, without going too much over the speed limit; getting a ticket would just make her even later, and that's the last thing she would want to happen. The fluffy, white clouds rolled passed her windows through the bright, orange sky. The sun was halfway risen, and Mi Cha could see the round orb of fire floating just above the horizon ahead. A smaller orb of yellow color was floating above Mi Cha's car as she drove right under it before it turned red. She took a right turn at the next light and drove to the end of the road, where her school was located.

When Mi Cha pulled into the parking lot, she noticed that a lot of cars were already there, and almost all of the parking spots were taken up. She was forced to turn into a spot that was pretty far from the entrance doors. She rolled her eyes as she shifted the car into park, then grabbed her backpack and jogged to the front doors.

She pulled out her phone and checked the time as she entered inside—7:32, two minutes late. She glanced up at the attendance lady, who was sitting behind a wall of glass. The lady looked down at her own watch and then waved her hand for Mi Cha to go on ahead.

The hallways of the school were filled with other students, both walking past and standing at their lockers. Some of them were casually talking, others were alone and grabbing their materials for the day. Mi Cha walked down the hall and around the corner, where her own locker was, and began to turn the combination dial. She opened it and began to grab a few things as somebody came up to her from the side.

"Hey, Mi Cha." The person said.

Mi Cha turned her head to see the dark, gelled hair and hazel brown eyes of Anthony.

"Hey."

"You, um…glad to be back at school?"

"No." Mi Cha let out a laugh that was mostly a sigh. "Are you?"

"I think it might help to get my mind off of some things."

"That's true."

"So, um…I don't want this to come off as too much or too fast, but uh...I was just wondering, you know, it's been over a week now, and we haven't really seen each other at all, so…well, I was just wondering if you would like to do something later tonight after school. Ah, not like a date or anything, but just to go hangout somewhere?"

Mi Cha zipped up her backpack and slammed her locker shut. "I can't, my family and I are going over to Dennis and Amber's for dinner."

"Oh, okay….that's fine. I understand."

"But there's nothing going on tomorrow night." Mi Cha let out a small smile and then leaned over and kissed Anthony's cheek before walking off to her first class.

6:00 PM

The sun was just beginning to change from its bright yellow glow, to a softer, orange hue as dinner time approached. Amber closed the shades over the kitchen window, which was now fixed from when Browden had smashed it. She was dressed in a long, white velvet dress with stockings underneath. Her light blonde hair was straightened down to her back shoulder blades. She wore a soft amount of mascara over her eyes, with a hint of peach eyeshadow. Her lips were glossed over with a pale, pink color that shimmered in the light. She was moving back and forth between the kitchen cabinets and the dining room table, which was located in the room just through the hallway. The table was set with five large, round plates, each with a set of silverware and a napkin. Two candles were placed at each end of the table, with space in between for the platters of food.

Dennis emerged from his bedroom upstairs and walked down the stairs, to the kitchen. He was dressed in a white, button down shirt, with a black sports coat over it. Black dress pants covered his legs, and he wore only socks on his feet. When he entered the kitchen, he made his way over to the counter and grabbed a platter of sliced pork chops. He carried it over, into the dining room, where Amber was setting up glasses next to each of the plates.

"Well, you look nice tonight." Dennis said as he set the platter down on the center of the table.

"Is that to say I don't look nice every night?" Amber replied with a smile as she set the last glass down.

Dennis made his way over to her on the other side of the table and gave her a kiss.

"You look *especially* nice tonight." He said.

"So do you." Amber replied as she made her way back into the kitchen and grabbed a large bowl of steamed rice. The steam floated up from the surface as she walked it over, into the dining room, and set it next to the platter of pork. "You think they'll like pork?"

"Of course, who doesn't like pork?" Dennis replied. "Don't worry, they're going to love your food."

"I just want them to be happy. They deserve it after everything they've been through."

"We had to go through it all too." Dennis said as he brought out a bowl of fried potatoes.

"We're used to it, it's our job. They're just an innocent family. I can't imagine what kind of mental scar it all might have left on them."

"It'll make them stronger, just like it does to us. After every crazy investigation, we learn more and more and come out a stronger person than we were before."

"Well, I hope that's what it does to them. We'll see what kind of condition they're in once they get here."

Hyon, Mi Cha, and Nari exited their house and made their way to the car in the driveway. Hyon was wearing a long, red dress with black high heels, and her dark hair was curled at the ends. Mi Cha wore a white, strapless top, with a tight, black pencil skirt and heeled sandals; her light brown hair was completely straightened, and soft, smoky eye shadow colored her eyes. Nari wore a little pink dress that puffed out at the ends, with small white shoes. The three of them hopped into the car and Hyon pulled it out, onto the road to head to their dinner party.

The drive lasted only about twenty minutes until Hyon pulled the car up, onto the stone driveway of Dennis and Amber's house. Soft, solar lights lit up their path to the front of the garage doors. Hyon shifted the car into park and was the last one to leave the car, as Mi Cha and Nari ran right up to the front door. Mi Cha pressed the doorbell with her white nail-polished finger, and stood waiting with Nari right in front of her. As the door opened, the green eyes of Amber peaked around the corner and she opened her mouth in excited as she locked eyes with Mi Cha.

"There she is!" Amber said, as her and Mi Cha locked arms. "You look so pretty."

"So do you!" Mi Cha replied as she stepped into the house.

"And I don't believe we met personally yet." Amber said as Nari came inside. "I'm Amber, nice to meet you."

"Thank you for saving us." Nari replied with a big smile on her face.

"Oh, you're welcome. We love being able to keep people safe from harm."

"You're like a superhero!" Nari replied as she walked inside and made her way over to her sister.

Hyon appeared in the doorway next and spread out her arms when she saw Amber. "So nice to see you again." She said as they hugged.

"You too! Are you holding up well?" Amber asked.

"Oh, I'm just fine. I like to think about the present and the future, and forget the past. Nari is back with me here in the present, and things are looking good for the future, so I'm doing just fine." Hyon smiled as she walked inside the house, into the foyer.

Amber shut the door after everyone was inside and led them through the kitchen and into the dining room, where Dennis was waiting. He stood up from his chair as the Park family walked in. He made his way over to Hyon first and greeted her with a handshake.

"Glad to see you all looking happy and healthy." He said and then gave Mi Cha a hug around her shoulders.

"Great to see you again Dennis." Mi Cha smiled.

"It's Mr. Superhero!" Nari shouted out.

Dennis laughed and flexed his arms out in front of him. "When the city needs saving, Dennis-Man is there to do it!"

Amber rolled her eyes and laughed as she went over and pulled chairs out for everyone to sit on. Hyon and Nari sat on one side of the table, Mi Cha and Amber sat on the other side, and Dennis sat the head.

"Okay, who's hungry?" Amber asked after everyone was seated.

"Everything looks so delicious." Hyon said. "Thank you so much for doing all of this for us."

"Oh yes, I love pork chops!" Mi Cha said as she looked at the platter in front of her.

"Eat as much as you'd like!" Amber said with a smile, as everyone began to put the food on their plates.

11:00 PM

Hyon, Mi Cha, and Nari were lined up at the door as they were getting ready to leave.

They had stayed for a few hours after they finished dinner, hanging out and talking with Dennis and Amber. Hyon spoke about her life back in South Korea, and how her husband just left her and the kids one day, without ever coming back. Without him, she was unable to support the family with only her job at the dance studio, so she decided to move to the United States where she found a job working for a sales business. She had said that the day Nari was kidnapped was her first official day on the job after weeks of training; that's why she wasn't home. She explained the complete panic she had felt when she received Amber's call explaining what had happened, but that after a while she felt reassured that her case was in good hands.

"Just from your voice alone and how nicely and calmly you spoke to me, I could tell that you were going to take care of us." Hyon had said.

Dennis and Amber spoke about previous cases that they had, and Hyon was especially interested in the Bermuda case. They told her about the fight they had with Captain Wacks, and about how the island sunk. They also described how they first met each other, and how Amber's old boyfriend had died through the Bermuda triangle; she was just finishing up her forensic schooling and was on

vacation, when her boyfriend went missing and that was when she met Dennis at the hotel. From then on, they worked together to solve the case. They both said that they knew they had a strong connection because of how well they were able to work together, despite having just met.

"It was as if we had been partners for years." Dennis had said.

They then went on to explain that they have their hearing coming up soon to testify for what happened during the mission, and that they are publishing a journal documenting it all. Hyon listened to their story with great interest and admired the two of them even more after hearing their great effort to uncover the mysteries of the Bermuda Triangle.

"To keep putting your lives on the line, just to help other people and solve cases," Hyon had said, "that makes me look up to you both with great honor."

After they had finished their stories and drank most of their coffee, Hyon stood up from the living room couch and thanked Dennis and Amber for inviting them.

"Well, it's getting pretty late, so we better get going now." She said as Mi Cha and Nari stood up with her. "Thank you so much for having us over. The food was great and it was so interesting hearing your stories."

"Oh, no problem at all. Feel free to stop by again sometime." Amber said as she stood up to give the three of them goodbye hugs.

After saying their goodbyes, the three of them made their way outside into the cool, nighttime air. It was

dark out, but Hyon could faintly make out the shadowy outline of her car. She walked over to it and opened the door, and the lights from the inside turned on. The light made a faint illumination around the driveway, so Mi Cha and Nari were able to see where they were going. Mi Cha came to the car first, and opened the door for Nari to climb in the back, then she opened the passenger's side and sat down next to her mom.

The drive back seemed quick through the quiet, empty, nighttime streets. Soft, orange glows from the street lamps bounced past their car windows as they drove by a few blocks to get back to their street. Hyon drove down to the end of the road, just before the last intersection, and pulled up, into her driveway. After she parked and shut the lights off, she made her way to the back door of the car and grabbed Nari's hand. She led her up the dark walkway to the front door. Mi Cha followed behind, using the light from her phone to see the ground better.

Hyon flicked on the light switch as soon as they entered the house. The couch and coffee table appeared out of the darkness as the lights lit up their living room.

"Why don't you go get your pajamas on and brush your teeth, then come to bed? It's a little past your bedtime." Hyon said to Nari as she let go of her hand.

"I want to sleep in my own bed tonight." Nari replied.

Hyon walked forward and set her purse down on the coffee table. "You sure? You won't be too scared to sleep alone again?"

"Nope. Dennis and Amber said if anything bad happens I can just give them a call and they'll come help."

"Okay sweetie. I'll leave my door open just in case you decide to come to my bed."

"Come tuck me in and I'll sleep like a baby." Nari replied as she made her way to the stairs.

"You *are* a baby still." Mi Cha said as they both went upstairs.

"Am not! I'm almost six!"

After Nari finished brushing her teeth and getting her pajamas on, Hyon entered her bedroom and walked over to pull down her bed covers. Nari hopped up and laid down on her back, and adjusted the pillow behind her head.

"All cozy?" Hyon said as she pulled the covers over the top of Nari's body.

Nari's head turned to the side as her eyes widened. Her mouth opened in a circle as she sat up in the bed and pointed a finger over to the corner of the room, near the closest. "Mommy! Help! It's gonna come for me! Get it away, get it away!"

Hyon opened her mouth in a gasp as she followed the direction of Nari's finger to the corner of the room, where a pile of stuffed animals were sitting. In the middle of the pile, she saw the long, droopy ears, round oval eyes, pink nose, and the white cotton tail of a stuffed rabbit. It sat there in the pile, with its black eyes in a fixed gaze, staring straight at Nari.

Hyon lifted herself slowly from her kneeling position at the bedside and walked over to the corner. She carefully bent down and picked the rabbit up in her hands. The purple fur felt soft and warm in her palms.

"No worries, sweetie." She said. "This one I remember buying for you a few years ago. But I think it's best if we do without it."

"I don't want it!" Nari shouted.

"I'll throw it out right after I tuck you in. Ah, crap, that's right. I completely forgot to take the trash out earlier." Hyon set the purple rabbit down onto the floor, then made her way back to the side of Nari's bed.

Nari laid back down onto the soft mattress and rested her head on the pillow. Hyon pulled the blankets up to Nari's shoulders and tucked them tightly underneath her body. She ran her hand through Nari's soft, brown hair and planted a kiss on her forehead.

"Goodnight Nari, I'll see you in the morning."

"Goodnight Mommy." Nari replied, as Hyon picked the rabbit back up and left the bedroom, leaving the door slightly cracked open.

Hyon looked to the left down the hallway and saw that Mi Cha's door was closed, and that her lights were off as well. She made her way down the stairs; they creaked softly in the quiet house as she stepped on them. As she came into the kitchen, she pulled open the lid of the trashcan and stuffed the purple rabbit inside. She lifted the

white, plastic bag out of the bin and made her way through the door, into the garage.

The garage door slowly creaked open as Hyon stood with her hand on the large handle of the trash bin; it was filled right to the top. The night sky was dark, but the light from her garage illuminated her driveway, as she walked down to the end of it with the trash bin. She stood it upright at the bottom corner near the road and turned around to head back, when a car pulled into the other driveway, just a few feet away.

Hyon grabbed the second bin of cardboards by the two handles and began to walk it down the driveway, as a man got out from the car next door and ran over to her. His hair was short and wavy and dark brown in color, with a few grays on the sides. His face was clean shaven, and he was wearing a dress shirt.

"Hey, let me help you with that." The man said as he took the bin off from her hands.

"Oh, thank you so much. Uh, what's your name? I know you just moved in next door a few weeks ago."

"Yeah, it's Andy. And yours?"

"Hyon."

"Hyon," Andy repeated, still holding the trash bin, "is that Korean?"

"I just moved here to the US about a month ago."

"Ah, nice. So don't you have a husband to help you take all this trash out?"

Hyon shook her head. "Nope. He, uh…he just left me and my kids one day. Never came back."

"Oh man, I'm so sorry to hear that." Andy said and then carried the trash bin to the end of the driveway, next to the other one. He walked back up in front of Hyon after he set it down. "Hey, if you ever need any help with any more household chores, just give me a call."

Hyon smiled and nodded her head. "I will, thank you." She said and then started to turn back towards the garage.

"Hey wait." Andy said as he took a few steps forward.

"What?"

"You can't give me call unless you have my number." Andy said with a smile.

Hyon smiled back and reached into her coat pocket to pull out her phone. She plugged Andy's number into her contacts before he wished her a goodnight. Hyon watched him as he walked back to his own driveway and entered the dark house. After he went inside, she turned her head back down to her phone, which had his number displayed next to his name. She smiled to herself once again, as she replaced the phone into her coat pocket and made her way back inside. The garage door squeaked to a close as she made her way upstairs to bed.

2:00 PM

"Is everything all set?" Dennis turned to the lady next to him and said. She was wearing large, eye glasses and her hair was tied up in a bun.

"All right here, sir." The lady handed him a bounded copy of a journal. "I have the important pages that I believe will be most useful during the hearing marked off for you. Of course, you aren't bound to stick to those pages. I just marked them for easy reference."

"Thank you, Rebecca."

"Here's one for you too ma'am." The lady with the bun handed another copy of the journal to Amber.

Dennis and Amber were standing in the hallway outside of the court room. They were waiting to be called in for their hearing. Dennis was dressed in a dressy black suit, and Amber wore a tight black skirt, with a black jacket over a white blouse. She held the book in between her hands and tapped her fingers nervously over the back cover.

"We just have to go in there and present the facts of the case. As long as we tell the truth, there's nothing to be nervous about."

"I'm just worried that they won't believe us." Amber replied to Dennis.

"That's what we have this journal for." Dennis held up the book. "This is a primary source that I documented. The judge can't call into question my memory since I wrote everything down as it happened throughout those two months."

"There's nothing to *prove* that it was written then."

Dennis lowered the journal with one hand and reached his other hand out, onto Amber's shoulder. "Look, the entire island of Bermuda is gone, that obviously isn't a normal occurrence. So the judge won't be expecting a normal answer. I'm sure he knows it's going to be something crazy."

"But will he be expecting something THIS crazy?"

Dennis shrugged his shoulders, then turned towards the courtroom doors as somebody walked out.

"The judge is ready for you two." The man said, as he waved his hands for Dennis and Amber to step inside.

The court room was filled with people; they packed the seats tightly like sardines, while some were even standing around the walls. People with TV cameras were set up by the front of the room, next to the judge's podium. Dennis and Amber walked side by side up the narrow aisle, as the cameras turned their attention on them. People snapped pictures with their cameras and cellphones, and some people began to cheer loudly and applaud the two of them. Everyone there had seen the news the week before about the saved children, and they looked up to Dennis and Amber as heroes. Dennis flashed smiles and waved at some of the people, and at the cameras, as he continued to walk with Amber up to the table at the front, where Director Hanzel was waiting for them.

As they were halfway up the aisle, Dennis felt something touch his arm. It was the warm, soft press of a hand. He looked to his left and saw the light brown eyes of Mi Cha sitting in one of the rows of seats, next to Hyon, who had Nari in her lap.

"We're here to support you. Good luck!" Mi Cha said quietly, and Dennis flashed a smile at the three of them.

Amber approached the table first, and made her way to the seat in the middle, next to Director Hanzel. Hanzel had the front of her light gray hair tied up, while the back was hung down. She wore a dark gray sweater with a black skirt and stockings. Thin, black framed glasses covered her eyes, as she had her head down sorting a few files. Dennis took the last seat at the table, right next to the aisle.

"Okay, time to get started." The judge said and then banged the gavel. The people in the crowd quieted down as he spoke. "I know everyone here is very grateful to you both for the work you have done with saving the kidnapped children last week, and I applaud you for that as well. However, let us not allow that to distract us from the main point of focus here today. This court hearing is about a case you had from about a year ago. The Bermuda case."

The judge rolled up the sleeves on his black robe and flipped a piece of paper over that was sitting on his podium.

"Now, it says here that Commander Layton was the one in charge of the case at the time, however, I have heard the news of his killing, and I am very sorry to hear that. We instead brought FBI Director Hanzel here to help testify, as she is technically in charge of all cases. So, Director, if you would please state the reason for starting the Bermuda investigation in the first place, and who you assigned the mission to."

Director Hanzel looked up at the judge and held her glasses in one hand as she spoke. "There were many reports of ship and plane disappearances after having traveled around the Bermuda triangle. I sent Commander Fischer, who was only an Agent at the time, along with the late Lieutenant Vira to the island to investigate."

"Okay, so Ms. Berns here was *not* formally assigned to the investigation, correct?"

"That is right."

"Alright. So Ms. Berns still worked with Mr. Fischer on the case, despite her not having officially joined the FBI until *after* the case?"

"Yes, that is right."

"That does raise a little bit of concern for me."

"Your honor, the bureau was not aware of Ms. Berns' role during the investigation. Any help that she did put in was completely by Mr. Fischer's judgement of how to best handle the situation."

"Understood. It is not against any laws for an agent to obtain assistance from outside sources. Perhaps

when I hear more about the case I can better understand why Ms. Berns was assisting though."

Director Hanzel nodded and sat back down in her chair.

"Okay, with all that said, I think it's finally time." The judge said as he looked up from his papers. "Mr. Fischer, if you would, please tell us your story."

Dennis gave a quick glance, and a smile, to Amber and Director Hanzel. He stood up and turned his head towards everybody in the audience, towards the cameras, and then finally back towards the judge.

"Your honor, in order to better tell the story of Bermuda, I present to you, and to everybody here in the court room today, this journal. It was written by me, as a primary source for my entire investigation there on the island." He held up the journal in his hands with the cover facing outward, so that the judge and cameras could see it. "This…this is the story of Bermuda."

The End

Order BERMUDA: Buy Now Lulu

Lulu.com/spotlight/dylanasfur

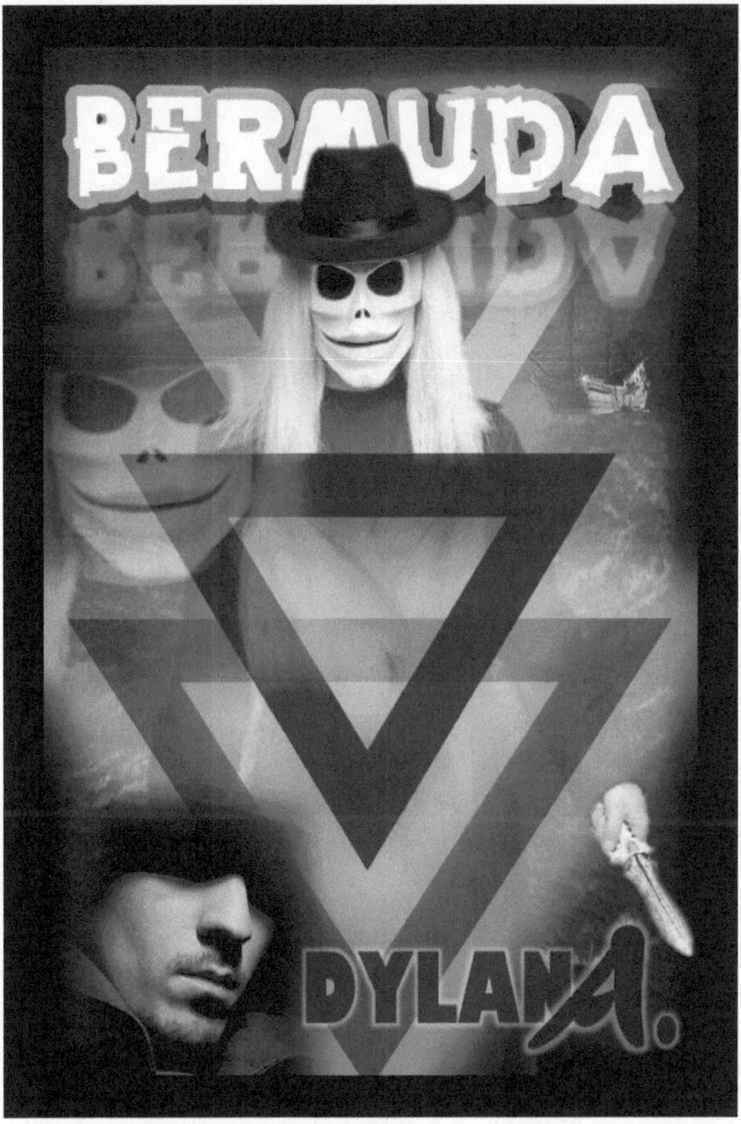

ABOUT THE AUTHOR

DYLAN A.

Full Name: Dylan Asfur

YouTube: @dylanasfur

Instagram: @dylanasfur7

Twitter: @asfurd

ABOUT THE AUTHOR

Hello, I am Dylan A. and I am 18 years old at the time of this book's publication. I have lived in upstate New York for my entire life so far, and have recently began studying film and writing at Bard College. I plan to continue with my writing and video making on my YouTube channel because it is what I most enjoy doing. The idea of creating something of my own work that others can enjoy and be entertained by, is always a great feeling. It's very humbling that my work can entertain and make other people happy.

I have always loved writing since I was about 5, and I grew up mostly on R.L Stine's Goosebumps books. I've always loved dark and scary movies, as my favorite genre. Something about it just captivates me more so than any other type of film. I also love crime and investigative type shows, which is why I like to combine the two styles for my own books. This genre can be both super fun to read, while still containing substance and professional literary elements throughout it; and that's exactly what I strive for in my writing.

As another fun fact, if you don't know my YouTube channel at all, I am a huge KPOP fan and love to do reaction and unboxing videos. My favorite artist is CL and my favorite group currently is BlackPink. I also do gaming and challenge videos on my channel, as well as short films and music videos. Hope you check it out and subscribe to become an **A.gent**!

Made in United States
Troutdale, OR
11/15/2023